Voyage to the End of

TIME

To James & Margaret

Joe Fitzpatrick

Great Friends

Voyage to the End of

TIME

A NOVEL

Joe Fitzpatrick

TATE PUBLISHING
AND ENTERPRISES, LLC

Published by Tate Publishing & Enterprises, LLC
127 E. Trade Center Terrace | Mustang, Oklahoma 73064 USA
1.888.361.9473 | www.tatepublishing.com

Tate Publishing is committed to excellence in the publishing industry. The company reflects the philosophy established by the founders, based on Psalm 68:11,
"The Lord gave the word and great was the company of those who published it."

Published in the United States of America

ISBN: 978-1-61862-048-4
1. Fiction / Science Fiction / Space Opera
2. Fiction / Science Fiction / Romance
12.01.03

Dedication

This book is dedicated to my wife, Barbara, who for the last forty-five years has inspired me to use my God-given talents to pursue my dream of writing.

Also, my appreciation to the thousands of students I taught over a forty-year period. I hope you read this book and remember all the stories I told you in science class. You might not have understood the science concept; however, from what you have told me as we have aged, all of you remember that as long as you can relate something to a story, it stays with you forever. The same is true for all the books you read.

And a big thanks to David Bearman for reading the contract and to Sylvia LaHue for editing the grammatical errors.

Preface

The following scenario began as a dream, only to unfold into a cosmic exploration of the universe. The year was AD 2760, and life in Galaxy Fourteen was busy, never a moment to idle away time with a game of poker or chess. Galaxy Fourteen consisted of nineteen planets, each dependent on the other for supplies and communication to Central Intelligence. Wars were non-existent, and people responded to one governmental body. The galaxy was one under the Unification Treaty of Planets.

Everyone lived in space housing with few ethnic differences as to race, creed, or color. Medical procedures, cures for diseases, and medications to combat all types of illnesses had progressed at an unimaginable rate. Everyone was somewhat immune to most communicable and contagious diseases.

The food supply consisted of high-protein food capsules, including an ample supply of vitamins and liquids. Most people were exceedingly healthy and enjoyed an abundance of recreational activities. Scientists and researchers were always attempting to identify meaningful ways of probing into the depths of outer space. Transportation was accomplished through the use of teleporters that enabled people to quickly move from one location to another. As a result of seismic and climatic changes, people were forced to evacuate the planet Earth and form colonies in other galaxies.

The Mission

My heart raced with anticipation as plans were finalized by Captain Vick for the next day's journey aboard the spaceship *Fanfare*. Would my name be selected as one of those to participate in the mission? I knew little about the voyage, except that several hundred people were being chosen to explore other galaxies and attempt to make contact with different civilizations.

I felt sure that my best friend, Steve Matthews, would be selected to go on the voyage. He and I had known each other most of our lives.

"Hey, Kit, what are you doing sitting here all alone by the window?" Steve asked.

"Oh, I'm thinking about the next group of passengers to be teleported to Galaxy Fifteen by means of the marvel ray. I just wonder how the transition will occur when each person's molecular structure is interwoven in a long chain, forming a pattern that moves from galaxy to galaxy."

"I have wondered the same thing myself."

"Steve, you know how I've always taken time to pray when pressure was mounting in my studies or I felt alone and downhearted from being disciplined. I missed having parents when I was assigned to that children's ward at about the age of seven. I can't remember how I got completely separated from my parents, but obviously it was some type of emergency situation or they would never have abandoned me."

"Kit, don't berate yourself."

"Every time I faced insurmountable consequences at the children's ward, I prayed to the Lord God for guidance and to help me find my purpose in life. I always felt comforted knowing there was someone who would listen and guide me. The best day of my life was when we became friends."

"Steve, both of us have been career officers for the National Space Agency for quite some time. You know, my one disappointment thus far in life is that I have been unable to find a perfect mate with whom to spend my life. We are both so busy with all the activities and studying we have to do that there seems to be no extra time to meet someone and explore the possibility of a life together. Do you feel the same way?"

"Yes, there are times when I feel so alone, and I know I'm getting older. With the possibility of our being selected for this important voyage, I am excited about it, but somewhat apprehensive at the same time. Kit, I know you have great faith in God. Put your trust in him, and keep praying that he will enable you to find the love of your life. For the time being, let's just remain the best of friends and let God plan our futures for us. I've got to run now, as I need to be packed if my name is called for the mission."

"Okay, Steve. I'll catch up with you later."

At the young age of seventeen, I began my career at Central Intelligence in the year AD 2748. Having a knack for ingenious ideas that could be applied to space technology, my education included experimentation for the advancement of space vehicles. Our purpose was to find ways of traveling through space at a velocity and acceleration rate that far exceeded anything in the universe.

My thoughts began to focus on the next group of people to embark on a space mission. I noticed everyone who was about to leave had a gleam in their eyes and seemed quite happy to pursue an unknown mission.

All at once I heard my name being called over the sound system. "Kit Bartusch, space engineer, report to Module Twelve for mission assignments right away! There you will be given specific orders and directed to join the crew members in the main control room of the spacecraft."

Scared! Excited! Afraid! All those feelings were running rampant in my mind. Now that I knew I would be part of an elite group of space explorers, I thought about the challenges we would face during the journey. *Will we encounter more advanced civilizations in unchartered territory? Are we prepared to defend ourselves if need be? Will communication be a problem? If we are fortunate to locate other civilizations, will they accept us as friends or foes?*

Fear of the unknown and the feeling that I might never be able to return to my home in Galaxy Fourteen were now uppermost in my thoughts. The one constant in my life was my faith in God that had been instilled in me since childhood. Another concern was how other civilizations might react to my belief in God. Would they even know anything about God? I wondered if the voyage would change my life forever.

All at once I heard over the speaker, "Steve Matthews, space engineer, report to Module Twelve for mission assignments." I was so glad to know that my friend had also been selected for the mission.

A rigid schedule had been designed to determine the orbital path that the exploration rocket ship was to follow during its flight. Speed was also a major factor in order to avoid collision with meteoritic rocks in Galaxy Seventeen, which represented man's farthest attempt to probe outer space. To bypass Galaxy Seventeen, the spaceship had to maneuver the meteoritic belt that clung in its gravitational field successfully.

That night in Module Seven, I had a surreal dream. From the depths of my subconscious mind, I perceived the future before me. A group of people known as the New Empire would make the laws, provide defense, and govern people from all planets. How was it possible that I, an insignificant space scientist, could see so far into the future?

As I lay there, I saw myself being transported through time by means of a cerebral telemeter that brought one's spirit into whatever zone of time was desired. I found myself in a place so different from Galaxy Fourteen that I was actually frightened for a moment. There was a wooded area beside a flowing stream. I began to walk through the woods until I came to a clearing. Before me was the most beautiful gold city imaginable. Gleaming brightly, it was not the typical structure of our space cities back home but more like early twentieth-century architecture.

I stood there in total awe and looked at the massive structures. As I walked toward the city, I found a road, somewhat metallic in substance, yet it reflected no light or heat. Tracks, like for a railroad, were obvious; however, there were no ties for a train track. My mathematical mind deduced the fact that railroads had been out of date for over seven hundred years. I continued toward the city. As I walked, I realized that my body felt different. I became very concerned as my head began to hurt. My arms were tingling, and then I fainted.

I awakened and found myself in a strange building that appeared to be of early Roman architecture. There were art carvings of gold and silver and pictures of dignitaries lining the walls. I was not harmed and seemed to be okay physically. The condition of my clothing was the same metallic sheen covered in red and embossed in gold and silver.

What did seem odd was that the room in this building had oval windows and a partially oval-type entrance. The room was covered with oriental tapestries that hung from each of the four walls, and the ceiling had a mirrored effect. I walked over to one of the windows and looked out at the horizon that was covered with a network of buildings forming a metropolis.

People moved in what appeared to be a mall-like structure by using moving platforms embedded in the space provided for walking. Sporadic movement indicated they got on and off randomly. The one thing that surprised me was the absence of sound, sinister to behold. It was as if time stood still as I peered out the window.

Suddenly, I heard an earthly voice, and standing before me was a military group of officers. With a military salute, the leader said, "I'm Captain Alsac. Welcome to our planet. Do not be frightened. We mean you no harm and ask that you follow us."

Having no choice, I walked with them down a hallway until we came to a large chamber filled with formally dressed people.

At the end of the hallway was a king. We proceeded along until we suddenly stopped, and the king motioned me to come toward him. He had a rather large physique, dark hair, and was at least six feet, six inches tall. Four people were standing beside him, presumably his wife, daughter, and two sons.

"It is good to meet you. Let me introduce myself. I'm Cantor, King of the New Empire."

"Hello, sir. I'm Lieutenant Kit Bartusch."

"Lieutenant, where did you come from and what is your purpose in being here?"

"Well, Cantor, I'm from Galaxy Fourteen. I'm involved in space exploration, and my travels have led me here."

My appearance seemed much the same as his, although our clothes differed. While mine were more metallic, his family's attire appeared to be made from a very expensive, imported silk fabric.

Staring at me in a mystic sort of way, Cantor motioned for me to accompany him to a private room for further discussion. After being seated, he at once asked me to recite my name and purpose for being transported to his planet.

"My name is Kit Bartusch, a space engineer for Central Intelligence from Galaxy Fourteen."

"Kit, I've never heard of this Galaxy Fourteen. Where is it located?"

"Cantor, we are located approximately two hundred light years from the Milky Way Galaxy. Our purpose in exploration of space is to make contact with alien civilizations and extend our boundaries. We mean you no harm." Thankfully, my explanation seemed to satisfy him.

I then looked directly at Cantor and asked him to explain to me where I was in relation to my own galaxy.

"Well, Kit, the area we are currently in is the nucleus of the New Empire, the unification of civilizations and planets in this Galaxy. You must understand that we are extremely advanced in both the study of science and space travel. All our operations are highly technological."

"Your description is enlightening Cantor. However, when I departed from Galaxy Fourteen, the year was AD 2748. Could you tell me what year this is?"

"By our current calculations, the year is AD 3250."

I immediately knew I must have traveled through some type of time zone. Needless to say, I was confused that a phenomenon such as this could happen. According to Cantor, the New Empire was formed by the union of galaxies two hundred seventy-five light-years from the Milky Way Galaxy.

The galaxies included Andromeda, Cuerva, Tacirus, and Libracanus Marcusan. All these names were beyond my realm of knowledge. Here I was some two hundred light-years away from my own galaxy in another time dimension. Somewhat frightened, *I wondered if I would ever see Galaxy Fourteen again.*

After our brief meeting, I was returned to my assigned quarters by Commander Alsac and supplied dinner via a painless twelve-second heat ray aimed from the ceiling toward my body.

"Commander Alsac, are you sure this procedure of securing food will not harm me?"

"Of course not, Kit. The molecular structure of the ray provides necessary nourishment to sustenance of life and the body receives the energy very well."

Strangely enough, I felt full, as though I had consumed two space food capsules. I then lay down and immediately fell asleep.

The next morning, Commander Alsac took me to meet the mayor, and they escorted me on a tour of the city. They informed me the population was approximately twenty-six million people. The New Empire was similar in architecture to our space cities, and the temperature was comparable to a region of sub-humid climate.

As we walked, I suddenly saw someone dangling helplessly from a large scaffolding on a building nearby. Although I was on a tour of the city this person was in danger, and no one seemed to notice. Commander Alsac and I left the tour, and I immediately turned on my teleporter. As it *vroomed* to life, powering on, I set my location for the top of the scaffolding with the push of a button. Materializing quickly at the top of the building, I ran to the edge, looking for a way to grab onto this poor soul.

"Give me your hand!" I shouted.

A rough-looking but definitely female hand reached out to me. *A girl? Why would a girl be working at a building site,* I thought as I grabbed her flailing limb.

"Thank you so much!" the young lady said. I tensed my arms and pulled her up until she could reach the scaffold's edge with her work boots.

"Hold onto me, young lady, as I use my teleporter to lower us safely to the ground."

"No, no! I'm afraid!" she screamed.

In a reassuring tone of voice, I touched her hand and said, "You will be safe."

"Watch as I demonstrate what happens." As I activated the teleporter, I stepped off the building and stood motionless in midair.

"I can't believe you are not touching anything, and you aren't falling."

"Do you now see that my device is safe?" I asked her.

"Yes, I'm impressed but still frightened."

"Put your trust in me, and I'll get us safely to the ground," I said.

As I moved closer to her, attempting to alleviate some of her fear, I said, "Grasp my arms, and I will teleport us downward."

I knew I had to move quickly once she took hold of my arms in what resembled a death grip. In less than a minute we landed safely.

The crowd that had gathered to watch the rescue all wanted to ask questions; however, Commander Alsac ordered them to return to work.

"Sir, I don't know who you are, but that was a unique experience—one I will remember always. Thank you for saving my life," the girl said.

A cold chill ran through my body, and I suddenly felt I knew the girl from somewhere in my past. As she left with some other people, Commander Alsac, who had watched the miraculous rescue, suggested we sit down for a few minutes.

"Kit, I can tell you were perplexed once you realized the person working on the building was a female. In order to be accepted by the people who reside on this planet, you must understand that we have specific guidelines for employment in this galaxy. Only the well educated and those who have advanced technical skills in the maintenance and advancement of the New Empire are allowed to work in specific areas. I don't know about your galaxy, but females are as much a part of the work force as the men are here.

Immediately, a feeling of weakness overcame me, and I fainted. The next thing I remember, I was awake and back home in Galaxy Fourteen. Quickly I looked around to see if I was really home. *Everything looks the same,* I thought, *but the dream is so realistic.*

Space Voyage

That afternoon I walked to headquarters and received my new orders. I was to be placed in charge of space communications aboard the rocket ship *Fanfare*. I had heard reports of this craft and how it was designed to search for new galaxies. The mission was to proceed during the next seven years to the darkest reaches of space.

With extreme joy, I was promoted to the rank of lieutenant. Expectations and instructions intensified, as we were to leave in eighteen hours. Being a bachelor with no strings attached, the time factor was not an issue for me.

As I approached the *Fanfare*, I was shocked. It was not a rocket ship, but a type of flying saucer, so enormous it could enclose a small coliseum with ten thousand people inside. The spacecraft was magnificent and quite detailed, even down to the landing pods. I was ecstatic to be part of the crew of this scientific voyage.

As I climbed into the saucer, I could clearly see the intense fabrication of structure and complex metalwork of the rooms. It was actually a small city within itself. I was then elevated to flight control. Being ranked fifth from the captain, I would be allowed to vote on major decisions regarding contact that would be made with alien beings on all the planets visited.

For the first time in my life, I was going to be part of a space exploration that exceeded anything I had accomplished thus far. We were to leave our galaxy and travel to the next one, some five light-years away, or twenty-nine trillion miles.

As we descended deep into space, I wondered if perhaps in my lifetime I might see the beginnings of the New Empire. I calculated that at our speed of 565,189 miles per hour, it would take exactly 68.75 days to reach our closest galaxy that had been named Butres Lettus because of its nature of phosphorescence. The galaxy seemed to be pulling me in a spiritual way, the beginning of an exciting ordeal.

We continued on the orbital flight plan I had devised with a schedule to link up with Butres Lettus' gravitational field in sixty days. During this time, life aboard the *Fanfare* was filled with normal idiosyncrasies that make up any ship's crew.

My closest associate was Steve Matthews, who was in charge of personnel and radio technology, second in command to the captain. He and I spent much of our time researching and planning the extended flight path.

For the first thirty days of our voyage, all went well as we journeyed into space.

"Kit, Are you still haunted by that recurring dream?"

"Yes, Steve. I can't seem to get the girl out of my mind. Somehow I know she's real."

While on the bridge of the spacecraft, I asked Steve, "How long do you think it will be before we reach our destination?"

"Who knows?" answered Steve. "We are traveling in unchartered territory. I think our only problem is the time it takes to send and receive messages from Galaxy Fourteen."

As scientists we knew that static was increasing as well as the outside temperature on the spacecraft. There had been no attempt to send us a message by other civilizations. Just at that moment, I noticed a red light flashing on the control panel. "Look, Steve, someone is trying to make contact with us. Listen to those weird sounds. Check the computer and see if we can clear up the static."

We worked for over an hour at the computers, and as we listened more carefully, we could hear beeping sounds, possibly a primitive form of code. "Steve, do you think these sounds could possibly be a specialized code from another planet?"

"It is possible, but one thing I do know, Kit, the computers can't decipher whether the message is a plea for help or just simple speech that's garbled and being sent from afar."

"Kit, did you send out the universal message to the point of origin?"

"Yes, Steve. If the aliens are intelligent, then they should know that the symbol π (pi) is representative of a higher order of intelligence. Will you continue working on the computer while I address another problem in the control room?"

"Sure, Steve, but don't stay too long. We need to try to translate this message, even if it takes us all night."

Then, approximately two hours later, we encountered a belt of meteorites moving toward us on a collision course. To avoid them, we tilted 145 degrees and then veered back on course. The angle now at which we would approach our destination would deepen our view of the solar system, which resembled something like the shape of a tiger. I was truly fascinated.

All at once Captain Vick announced, "Officers, all twelve of you, report to the control room immediately." Wondering what was going on, we quickly made our way to the area. Once there, Captain Vick informed us that we had each been assigned to a space hop, with eleven crewmembers. Our assignments were to land on designated planets. All of us were familiar with the space hops, as we had been trained extensively in their use as shuttles.

"Captain, could I ask you a question?"

"Sure, Kit."

"I was wondering why we are being asked to go and observe each of the planets."

"Our missions are designed for observation only. Neither you nor your crewmembers are to be involved with any type of confrontation or interference with the existing societies. If by chance you do make contact, be cordial and tolerant of their rules. You are leaders and representatives of the National Space Agency. Each space hop has been equipped with enough supplies to last two weeks. Are there any questions?"

"No, sir."

When we entered Butres Lettus's gravitational field, our scanner on the *Fanfare* indicated a chain of twenty-six planets. I decided my crew would descend on planet thirteen because of its probable ability for communication.

It took about a week for the other space hops to scan their assigned planet to assess the situation.

"Steve, did you read the reports from the first twelve planets?"

"Yes, Kit. We found evidence of what resembled primitive farming on most of the planets, and the soil from the scan indicated high nitrogen content sufficient to grow crops. As for inhabitants, our scanners failed to indicate any visible life forms."

With this analysis, we came to the conclusion that these planets were obviously food reserves for a large body of people.

As we approached the thirteenth planet, the temperature sensors continued to rise in the mother ship for unknown reasons. The intercom buzzed with static, and then I heard, "Lieutenant Bartusch, report to Captain Vick in space hop number five."

"At your command, sir."

"Gather your crew, board your space hop, and be prepared to blast off in thirty minutes."

With everyone boarded, we left the *Fanfare*, and within hours a planet could be seen. It was surrounded with a thick, gaseous atmosphere.

As we descended toward the surface, we turned on the scanners. To our surprise, glowing lights appeared on the horizon. *This sure looks modern.* We landed in an area resembling a large clearing of land with a magnificent city set on a hillside.

The planet was very similar to the one I was stationed on in Galaxy Fourteen, and for a while I almost thought I was home. We took atmospheric readings and found the chemical composition of the atmosphere to be 34 percent oxygen and 66 percent nitrogen. We knew from our extensive research that the percent composition of elements was slightly higher than our atmospheric air levels and tended to slow down biological activities in the exploration process. Our data also indicated temperature measurements that were near 80 degrees Fahrenheit.

As we started to depart the space hop, I heard the sound of many feet shuffling through the dirt. We looked up to find that we were surrounded by a body of people, silent, unarmed, and staring.

Are they hostile or peaceful? I thought, wondering how to proceed. Rather than coming out of the space hop, we spoke to them via intercom. "Greetings, people of this planet. We wish you no harm. We only wish to know the inhabitants and culture of this civilization. We have no intention of hostility."

Since our space hop's computer had the ability to convert ninety-six dialects into a comprehensible language, we assumed they would reply forthwith. But the faint buzz of the intercom produced no reply.

"Crew, did you notice how the people were dressed in those bright-colored outfits and how modern the buildings all looked?" *They must have thought we were a group of aliens dressed in our space hop uniforms.*

They showed little expression, neither sincerity nor doubt at our presence. For about an hour, most of the crew simply stared at the strangely dressed people. Our sensors indicated no hostile weapons anywhere within sixteen miles.

During my observation, I noticed a tingling sensation in my head. I felt uneasy and tense. "Help me, Steve. I feel dizzy and sick to my stomach. I've got to lie down."

"Kit, why don't you go to the back of the space hop, and I will send a crewman to give you some medicine to calm your stomach. I'll also notify the captain that you are ill."

Once the medication took effect, I felt better and began to think about the people we had just observed. All at once, I realized their form of communication was mental telepathy. From all indications, a shrill voice began piercing my mind in some form of communication with me.

"What's going on?" I asked.

"I am Lambda Photon, of the New Empire. The people before you are also inhabitants from a colony of the New Empire. We are very powerful, feared by many galaxies."

"Lambda Photon, we have not been sent here to harm you. A meeting will be arranged with a representative from our space hop to discuss peace relations and colonization. Are you agreeable to these arrangements?"

"That will be satisfactory. Let me know the time and place." *I'm sure I'll be the one sent.*

When I told the captain everything the alien had relayed to me, he replied, "We must know more before we place our men in danger."

I felt somewhat guilty, as I had been the one to receive the initial communication.

"Captain Vick, I would be honored to represent us, but first I must contact Lambda Photon by using mental telepathy instead of with an intercom system."

"Okay, try to contact her your way."

I sat and began to meditate and mentally make my connection. The first attempt failed, and I knew even more concentration would be required. After three trials, I heard a voice. I realized it was Lambda Photon issuing orders to be followed.

Space explorer from another planet—as you depart the space hop, you will find another alien being and myself waiting for you. Do not be afraid, and make sure you show no signs of resistance. The alien is trained to attack on my command.

I understand and assure you I will follow your orders.

As I stepped out of the space hop, I asked, "Are you Lambda Photon?"

"Yes, and who are you, sir?"

"I'm Lieutenant Kit Bartusch."

That's all she needs to know at present.

"I have been directed to escort you to our home base."

While she spoke, I observed her blonde hair and the fact that most of her body was covered with some type of uniform or defense suit. Accompanying her was a strange-looking creature that stood eight feet tall, and from tentacle to tentacle, it was six feet wide. With a cursory voice, she said, "Ignore my bodyguard or I will command it to hurt you."

I knew from our conversation that I had to follow her instructions if I wanted to succeed in the mission.

We walked over to a strange vehicle, boarded it, and strapped ourselves into the seats. The vehicle looked much like a car set on a platform that probably moved at a high rate of speed. There were no windows; however, some form of light was emitted from the roof. Wow! Such energy! The vehicle traveled quietly but swiftly to our destination in what seemed to be about three seconds. When we exited, I found we were inside a gorgeous city of gold and splendor. For a moment, I forgot where I was as I gazed at all the tall buildings and transportation vehicles. People were moving around everywhere, yet a feeling of peacefulness overcame me.

I was taken to a building, where we boarded an elevator that made a rapid descent. "Lieutenant Bartusch, just remain calm as we make our descent. In a matter of seconds we will be in the year AD 3250," Lambda Photon said.

"What is that intense pressure I feel? My chest hurts and I am having difficulty breathing." *What did she mean—the year AD 3250?*

"The elevator has been specially designed to resist the g-force produced by acceleration. The pressure will decrease as we reach our destination."

Upon exiting the elevator, to my amazement, there were lakes and streams, green lawns, and rolling hills. Everything that was happening was surreal. Why were we traveling into the future? I was curious and didn't have much patience when I needed answers. Lambda Photon just looked at me with a twinkle in her eyes and didn't say a word.

We walked a short distance until we came to a beautiful home set in a valley. From all appearances, the home was well fortified. As we approached the entrance leading to the house, we were blinded by an intense, white light. In what seemed to be mere seconds, we were inside the home. The interior resembled a mansion, much like where a general or admiral might live with numerous attendants.

Suddenly, a bearded alien, dressed in extremely bright clothing, appeared before us. Instead of using mental telepathy to communicate, he spoke in a familiar language. At once, I realized this being was Cantor. *Am I going crazy? Or perhaps I am in a dream state of mind.*

"Kit, you look somewhat perplexed. As King of this empire I want you to relax, as both you and my daughter are safe. The New Empire uses a powerful laser beam that can be projected to most solar systems using the libido of the mind for mental telepathy. *Now, I'm really lost. What in the world is he talking about and how does all this involve me?* Your mind was highly receptive to the test we performed. All other attempts to enter the minds of people have failed. You are our one and only success thus far. Within my grasp was a part of science so different and unusual that I was intrigued and wanted to learn specifics concerning my newfound knowledge.

The New Empire

I was then taken to Cantor's summer home as a guest for a few days. "Kit, as King of this Empire, I will now explain how all the things you have just experienced actually occurred."

Thank goodness for that, I thought.

"Several thousand years ago, scientists devised a way to transverse time so that their solar day was equivalent to an earthly hour. While you are here with us, you will be able to communicate with the space hop by using a specialized triple-beam laser, specially prepared for time travel. The mechanism has the capability of contacting people from the past, present, and future."

I felt more comfortable knowing that at any time I was provided with the means to communicate with my people.

During this time exhaustion overcame me, and Cantor had me shown to a room for rest. Upon awakening, I felt as though I had slept eight hours; however, according to my watch, only ten minutes had passed.

I immediately took out my communicator and tried to contact space hop five. No answer! Once again, I punched the necessary buttons. Still nothing! *Is my signal being jammed or is it possible I really am in the future?*

As I looked out the window, there was a formidable view of the surrounding countryside. All that had transpired seemed vastly impossible. I wondered, *Is my mind playing tricks on me?* While surveying my surroundings, I found the furnishings to be neoclassical yet with true splendor befitting a king. This was the kind of place everyone dreams of but never finds. *How I wish I could remain here forever, forgetting the past, living day to day.*

∞

In a little while, the king's courier brought a message from Lambda Photon inviting me to a dinner reception, where many important people would be in attendance. I was summoned at once to the Gala Ballroom.

Why am I being invited to participate in one of their parties? I thought.

I left and made my way down the corridor until I came to a large room half the size of a gymnasium. There were many strange-looking beings in the room, some very large and gruesome. All the aliens were dressed in radiant clothing indicating the richness of their planet. The females were dressed in gowns of silver splendor, decorated with expensive gems, most likely diamonds, rubies, emeralds, and sapphires.

An attendant approached me in a most suspicious way and said, "Sir, follow me."

As we made our way to the ballroom, I gave particular attention to the elaborate décor. The floor was like something out of a fairy tale—pink marble with black spiral lines. Gracing the walls were drapes in psychedelic colors. There were guest chairs along the walls that were similar to leather recliners. Adding to the festive surroundings were high-and low-pitched musical sounds that prompted those in attendance to participate in what appeared to be some form of unusual dance routine similar to early twentieth-century rock-n-roll.

As we reached the end of the hallway, I was greeted by Lambda Photon, who was dressed in a designer-type outfit that looked similar to the feminine clothing of Galaxy Fourteen. I immediately noticed there was something very intriguing about her. She always seemed to want to be with me and even showed signs of infatuation. Her attraction to me was captivating yet somewhat aloof.

"Isn't this a wonderful gathering, Kit? I hope you are enjoying yourself."

"Oh, yes, everything is lovely."

I noticed those on the dance floor were familiar with the various moves they were making, and I became uncomfortable.

Lambda Photon immediately asked, "Would you like to dance?"

"Oh, no, I would embarrass myself and you!"

"Don't be ridiculous, Kit. This is not a contest. Come on, we'll have a great time. Just listen to the music from the Galaxy Myrcanus Umbra. Take my hand and let's try the dance together. I'll help you." *Sure, I thought, it will be great for her, but I will make a big fool of myself. How can I say no when she is such a beautiful girl?* As time passed, I became even more fascinated with her.

As we moved onto the dance floor, we started to jerk, twist, and bend. We danced for at least two hours, and when the music stopped, we walked over to a table and sat down in the dimly lit room.

"Kit, let's walk out onto the terrace and look at all the stars in the sky."

Despite my physical attraction to her, there was something that made me extra cautious and always on guard.

"Kit, are you wondering why I like to spend so much of my time with you?"

Can she read my mind completely?

"I am Cantor's only daughter, and he is very protective of me. Daddy must feel that you are trustworthy, as he asked that I invite you to the ball, and I was delighted you accepted my invitation. Whether you realize it or not, we have not shielded you from the everyday occurrences on this planet, although you are from a distant world. You have seen things that no one else has had the opportunity of viewing. Besides that, I'm very attracted to you and enjoy spending time alone with you."

"Lambda Photon, there is something I must tell you," said Kit.

"Sure, what is it?"

"Do you remember being rescued from the tall building?"

"Of course! That was a terrifying ordeal."

"Well, I am the one who rescued you."

"Yes, I recognize you. I'm very impressed with the technology used to rescue me. In all my experiences, I've never seen anyone use such a device that enables a person to defy gravity."

"Lambda Photon, how did you know it was me?"

"Kit, I have highly developed extrasensory powers that enable me to read the minds of others provided they are on the same frequency and wavelength."

While gazing at the stars, Lambda Photon looked over at me and said, "Kit, I also need to ask you some questions, and I wonder if you will think I'm being rude with my inquiries."

"Ask me, and I'll answer if I can."

"First, I need to know from where you originated."

"That's easy—Galaxy Fourteen."

"Secondly, I need to know exactly what you are doing here."

How in the world am I ever going to explain that to her? "I am a representative of my homeland and have always been eager to make contact with other civilizations."

"Then, Kit, what are you planning to achieve on this mission?"

The mission? With all the excitement, I had almost forgotten about the mission. I thought for a moment. *How can I leave? Am I trapped here forever, or will I eventually return to my own galaxy?*

I could tell Lambda Photon's feelings for me were becoming more pronounced. As she gazed into my eyes and apparently forgot her question, she said, "Kit, promise me you'll never leave me."

"Lambda Photon, don't you think we need more time to get to know one another?"

"Kit, I'm frightened. Please don't shy away from me. You're my only hope."

What hope is she referring to?

"What are you afraid of, Lambda Photon?"

"I can't say at this time. Someone may be watching us."

"Lambda Photon, I'll be your constant companion for now. In the days ahead, it is possible that you may grow more attracted to me. However, currently, you hardly know me."

"Kit, I know enough about you to fall in love with you."

"Lambda Photon, I'm honored, but let's take things slowly and see what happens. I want you to know that I do like you. I just need some time to learn more about you and your culture."

"Kit, there will be plenty of time. You must stay close to me and put your trust in me."

I knew at that moment that God had answered my prayers. She had become the love of my life, so I looked into her glowing eyes and said, "I will never leave you."

I was enjoying myself and really felt comfortable in my surroundings. I turned to face Lambda Photon, but instead Cantor stood before me dressed in a long, flowing, silky robe of embroidered colors. He invited me inside to meet several guests.

As we re-entered the building, Cantor introduced me to the members of his family, including his gorgeous wife, Lycetius Myrvarka. His two sons, ages eighteen and twenty-one, didn't have much to say.

I was impressed with the members of Lambda Photon's family. Her mother and father sensed that she and I were becoming very close in our relationship. I knew I had to get to know her brothers and spend time with them. As a close-knit family, the siblings were more introverted than Lambda Photon but would speak when spoken to. If Cantor was speaking, they were quiet and followed his orders exactly. I did wonder about their clothing. They wore tunic-type outfits and both of them had some type of defense weapon around their waist at all times.

This concerned me; therefore, I asked Lambda Photon about the weapons, and she said, "Kit, we have always been taught to be prepared to defend ourselves at any given time. That is just part of our culture."

Lambda Photon, it turned out, was the only daughter, aged twenty-four. They were all friendly people who sensed my need for belonging, and I made friends quickly. The entire family seemed to be very polished and educated with good personalities and excellent manners. Lambda Photon had apparently told them about my background and galaxy of origin. They were impressed yet cautious, in an unsuspecting way.

After our initial meeting, I was invited to a private room for an elegant dinner. We were seated in an elaborate room that was decorated in extremely bright colors. I was surprised that everyone in attendance ate real food rather than capsules for energy. The meal was a new experience for me, as I had only read about and seen pictures of meat and vegetables back in Galaxy Fourteen. My food source had only been space capsules, a few nuts, fruits, and grains, as well as various liquids throughout my lifetime.

I was seated at a table beside Lambda Photon and noticed that several types of food had been prepared. A large portion of some strange type of meat sat beside

Cantor for him to serve. There was also an array of weird-looking vegetables with different-colored items resembling roots from plants sticking in all directions from the dish.

"Kit, don't be shy. Just try the different foods. I assure you that you will discover them to be both tasty and nutritious."

What am I going to do if I don't like the food? I can't insult her parents!

"I will try whatever you put on my plate, but make the servings small." Somehow I got through the meal and found a few of the items to be rather tasty. At the conclusion of dinner, we were also served some kind of sweet, red beverage.

After finishing the meal, we adjourned into a sunroom for additional conversation. Personally, I had been wined and dined, and no one had been alarmed at the arrival of a spaceman from Galaxy Fourteen. I wondered, *Why are they not suspicious of me?* No one seemed disturbed by my presence, and I was being treated as one of them.

Our next adventure was to watch a type of space television that projected a story of what Earth was like and the people who lived there. This scenario was comparable to one of those twentieth-century movies where the guy gets the girl and they live happily ever after. The aliens all seemed very interested in the Earth picture that centered on the family as a unit in society.

Looking in my direction, Cantor asked, "Are you enjoying yourself?"

"Yes, sir. It's been an interesting and fun night. You have all treated me just like a member of your family.

Thank you for dinner and your hospitality. Is it okay if I return to my room for the night?"

"Yes, Kit. We'll see you in the morning."

"Lambda Photon, would you like to walk with me?"

"Sure, Kit."

As we walked back to my room, Lambda Photon became more aggressive with her personal interest in me. She held my hand, and just before locking the door and leaving, she leaned toward me and kissed my cheek. Strangely, I felt completely safe, yet in an inconceivable way, I was gripped in fear—fear of what would become of me. *Everything seems to be going so great. I am in Cantor's house, so I don't think anything can possibly go wrong. Could I be mistaken?*

I got out my communicator and made another attempt to contact the space hop. "Calling space hop five. Come in." Nothing, absolutely nothing! *Communication with my crew is separated by time travel. That's why my communicator is failing. Even if I send a message, it will take a millennium to reach there. Totally useless.*

Underwater City

I lay down to rest, and time seemed to fly by. I dreamed all sorts of unimaginable things such as monsters chasing me, cannibals attacking me, and meteors striking the spaceship. Suddenly, I awakened and felt cold and clammy. My thoughts seemed so unrealistic at the moment. Surely, all that I had dreamed did not actually happen.

I got up and walked over to the terrace. There I was in another time, another place, and yet I felt so alone. Was I destined to be part of this life forever?

As I gazed out the window onto the terrace and grounds in the early morning hours, the sunlit planet seemed as beautiful as Galaxy Fourteen. There was only one thing that appeared very odd. Other than Cantor's immediate family, everywhere I looked there seemed to be an absence of human life.

I knew I was locked in and couldn't open the door, so I decided to climb out the window onto the terrace and walk on the well-manicured lawn. I turned around to see if anyone was watching, but I appeared to be alone. This seemed abnormal. I wondered, *Why is the entire area totally vacant? There is no one walking around. Where are all the people? This is so weird. Is something going on of which I am not aware?*

I started to walk around the magnificent building when I noticed that it exhibited a mirrored effect. It seemed as if the building were simply a mirage and intangible to the visual perspective. As I walked, I looked over my shoulder and saw a beautiful horizon completely filled with what appeared to be water as far as the eye could see. The sight was so surreal that I just stood there and absorbed the lovely surroundings.

For the moment, I didn't know what to think. I felt very confused. *Am I going crazy? I can see what appears to be a body of water in the distance; however, I can't hear any surf breaking on the shoreline. Maybe it isn't water. If not, what can it be? Is it possible that the scene before me is only a figment of my imagination?*

I suppose I had been looking out at this huge body of water for about fifteen minutes when I heard something move near me. My eyes scanned the area, but I saw absolutely nothing. It sounded like thundering drum beats in cut-time rhythm. *Something is moving toward me in the water.*

Suddenly, there appeared in front of me a mechanized water ship similar to a submarine. As I froze in my tracks, this multicolored object moved closer and closer to me.

Automatically it stopped, and a ray was beamed at my feet, similar to the teleporter ray in Galaxy Fourteen. Before I knew what had happened, I was transported inside the undersea craft into what appeared to be a stateroom for the very rich. Suddenly, I heard a loud voice on the speaker just above my head. "Spaceman, take a seat, and remain motionless until the undersea craft stops." All at once the craft moved downward very quickly. I noticed several portholes for viewing my surroundings and also realized that almost no sound came from inside the vessel.

There appeared to be no aliens aboard nor any exits for escape. The interior had a shape similar to space housing back home. For a few minutes, I almost thought I was inside a space module in Galaxy Fourteen.

I began thinking about everything that had happened to me, and I realized I must be considered an important person to be moved in this fashion from place to place. The undersea craft moved downward for at least fifteen minutes and then stopped. Stillness, quietness. I heard absolutely nothing for a while. Then a loud, booming sound erupted. I heard something that sounded like a door opening in the back of the undersea craft. The voice I had heard earlier got louder and louder.

"Spaceman, get up from your seat, and go into the adjoining room and sit down."

I guess that means me. So I got up, entered the other room and the door immediately shut. I wondered, *Is this to be the end of my existence on this planet?*

In all the excitement, I realized both hunger and thirst. I wanted to eat, and to my surprise, a table set with a feast was transported before me. It was at this point that I realized the people or aliens I was dealing with had developed an extrasensory perception far exceeding any predecessor.

Thoughts entered my mind as to why I should be hungry for food when all I was accustomed to was food energy transmitted through space food capsules. I suppose the food that I received in the New Empire was tasty, and the sensors in my brain likened to the taste.

As I began to eat, I scarcely noticed that the sea craft had stopped and docked. I peered out the window of this strange vessel and saw what appeared to be an underwater city. Although I only saw one side of a glass dome on the sea bottom, I assumed it must really be gigantic inside.

After consuming the food, I felt completely relaxed and to my astonishment, as my stomach settled, the food before me vanished. Was this a sudden figment of my imagination or a catastrophic happening of the mind linked perfectly with the subconscious?

Suddenly, my blood ran cold with fear—fear of the unknown. Out of nowhere came a paralyzing ray, holding me immobile. I was conscious of everything around me, yet I could not move. All at once, I heard something moving toward me. I looked around and saw nothing, yet the sound prevailed.

Like the flash of a camera, there appeared before me an array of exquisitely dressed people. Then, as quickly as I was paralyzed, I was released and completely surrounded by the aliens.

One of them motioned for me to follow him. Having no other choice, I did as I was asked. As I moved to another room in the vessel, I felt lightheaded, like I was moving without control of my human awareness. All at once, the alien pressed a lever on a light of some sort, and an opening in the side of the vessel appeared. As we walked through it, I knew I had experienced in previous time travel the same sensation of being physically raised into the air without touching anything. The pressure would hold me in check, thus preventing much motion. A feeling of complete motionless came over me, and I drifted in and out of consciousness before reaching my destination.

There I was, finally in the city of gold, yet so removed from human existence that I scarcely noticed the life around me. *Life? What life? Where am I?*

An attendant looked at me somewhat wearingly and told me to follow him as he escorted me to a bubble-type shelter. There, I was left alone. In observing my surroundings, I found all types of strange pictures illustrated with geometric polygons hanging on the walls.

I was tired, yet uneasy at the thought of being so alone. As I thought back over all that had transpired, I decided to rest and lie down on what appeared to be a cylindrical bubble. I had traveled so far and seen more than my mind could comprehend.

Amazing Discovery

Up to this point, no other time traveler had traversed the time barrier. It felt as if I had watched the hands of a clock move rapidly from one hour to the next. My mind kept going in circles. My body felt as if I was being drained of all my human resources and that everything I had done on this voyage was being replayed to me in my mind.

Suddenly, I sat up and looked at my watch. It had stopped. For how long, I didn't know. *I distinctly remember hearing the service engineer at Mission Control telling me my watch and other electronic devices were all checked and ready to go.*

This left me puzzled and ill at ease. I resolved myself to finding out what was going on. In my subconscious, I felt that very soon I was to become part of something big, so enormous that my mind would not let go of the thought.

A short while later I heard a barely audible voice telling me to come to the colored lining of the bubble. Then, right before my eyes, the bubble disappeared. It was as if I were standing inside the city on a moving platform. I thought I heard people walking and talking, yet I saw no one.

The thought did enter my head that I must be losing my mind. *Could this be real?* The platform carried me until I reached a large, shiny building that looked like gold. As an engineer, this style of architecture was of interest to me.

An opening appeared out of nowhere in the modernistic building. It so resembled all that I had read about of the lost city of Atlantis that I wanted to seek out some proof this was a genuine experience. Most of the buildings were shaped like the New Empire, and my imagination eluded me for the moment.

I went inside the building and walked down a long marble-floored hallway until I came to a room filled with people—my first encounter with civilization in this place. Up to this point, I felt neglected and dismayed at being left totally alone.

To my shock, there were Cantor and his family, including Lambda Photon. They all greeted me as if nothing had happened and I was back on the surface in his house. I kept my wits about me, acting calmly with an occasional suspicious glance from side to side.

I thought, *I feel as if I'm an escaped criminal returning to the warden of the prison. Why aren't the aliens angry for my disappearance and then reappearance? Regardless, I must not exhibit any fear if I want to survive in their environment.*

Cantor immediately invited me to a room that was secluded from the rest of the building. The area was exquisitely decorated with large, expensive tapestries on the wall. Strangely enough, I almost thought this was the same room I had occupied in Cantor's house.

"Welcome back, Kit. You have nothing to fear from us. Just relax," Cantor said.

How foolish I felt for having wandered away from his home and somehow being reunited with his family.

As Cantor looked directly at me, he said, "Kit, thousands of years ago there was a great civilization on the planet Earth. I know how unreal this may sound to you. It was located in my quadrant of space in the Milky Way Galaxy, not too distant from Galaxy Fourteen."

"Cantor, I have to ask if you are inferring the lost city of Atlantis on Earth?"

Cantor sat there in deep thought; however, he did not reply.

I remember my childhood dream of discovering Atlantis. Current research on the topic is extremely limited. From what I knew, exploration had been performed all over the planet Earth from the Island of Bimini, the Straits of Gibraltar, Greece, Sicily, and many parts of the Mediterranean Sea. In my dream world, I am the master who led archaeological expeditions trying desperately to uncover artifacts dating to the time of Atlantis. Having read and interpreted Plato's account of Atlantis, I am encouraged to dream even more about making such an enormous discovery.

How stilled my brain was that out of nowhere an entire race of people had moved from planet to planet until they found the necessary atmosphere for life. The idea was so inconceivable that a city such as this could completely disappear. I felt relief, knowing there was still some earthly matter that still existed.

Once again I asked, "Cantor, are you referring to the lost city of Atlantis?"

"That is a difficult one to answer, Kit. I have thought about it and will attempt to explain it to you the best way possible.

"Atlantis was a thriving culture, and the citizens were refined in the arts and sciences. As time went by, their population increased, thus creating a need for expansion. My ancestors were advanced scientifically and realized the need for additional colonization. The populace of my ancestors was very close knit and not inclined to accept others as easily as one might think. They built flying columns similar electronically to your teleporter device. As time elapsed, the city faced an even greater problem—seismic and volcanic activity. Because they knew they were facing insurmountable forces of nature, the scientists began preparations to construct a large craft to evacuate the people in order to vacate the planet.

"Kit, thousands of years ago, one of my ancestors was a brilliant scientist. While sitting at his drawing board one day, he sketched what appeared to be a powerful machine that could shrink the entire area of the city to a circle that was one hundred feet in diameter. By doing so, all twelve million inhabitants could eventually be transported from Earth to another planet."

I don't understand. How can a craft such as he describes transport all the people?

"In order for the plan to be successful, he also devised a blueprint for building a circular flying machine that could navigate through space at an untested velocity."

"How long did it take them to build the machine?"

"Altogether, it took them four and a half years to build the craft and ray machine and to assemble the people to leave for the new world."

"You know, Cantor, I might be able to visualize making the machine. However, it would need an enormous amount of fuel to go that far."

"Yes, that is correct, Kit. To fuel the spaceship, the people developed an electromagnetic propulsion system and an atomic particle of matter that had a half-life decay rate comparable to six and one half thousand years."

"Okay, I can go along with their development of the fuel, but what did they use for food?"

"Being such an advanced group of scientists, some were assigned the task of developing a dehydrated food supply that would last indefinitely."

"Cantor, your account of this event is almost like something out of a storybook."

"Yes, I know it sounds unbelievable, but the people of Atlantis knew their survival depended upon their ability to achieve their goals so they could be transported from Earth to another planet.

"According to the records, after all plans were finalized, the people were ecstatic with their accomplishments and set about the task of boarding the spaceship, leaving little behind that would indicate the city ever existed."

I suppose that is why no one ever found the city of Atlantis. "I can't imagine the enormity of such an endeavor. How long did it take them to reach their destination?"

"Kit, believe it or not, the craft moved through space at an incredible speed of two hundred thousand miles per hour. They had no choice other than to live on the spacecraft for two years before finally discovering a new solar system suitable for life."

"Cantor, once they landed, how did the people interact with the civilization already on the planet?"

"According to the records, it was difficult at first, as trust was an issue with so many people arriving all at once. It was total chaos. There were troubles with those on the planet, as they felt the new arrivals were trying to take over their planet. Eventually, they realized the people from Atlantis had superior methods of farming and the technology to develop materials, housing, transportation, and additional space adventures. In their favor was the fact they spoke so many different languages that communication was not a problem. As the two groups intermingled, a new society was formed, and they blended into one group known as the New Empire."

All this information sent my mind into overdrive. With my intuitive mind, I had to learn more about this historical event.

"Cantor, would you give me permission to read the manuscripts that cover all the scientific details?"

"Yes, I can arrange that for you, Kit."

I was taken to Cantor's personal library, where I found a most unusual sight. There were no books of any kind, only the most updated types of computers and other technological equipment that his assistant had to show me how to use. I was instructed to talk in any language to the computer, as it understood every word I would say. Incredible was not the word to describe how I felt as my questions were asked and the computer researched from an extensive database of material from all galaxies and then an answer was provided through a voice monitor.

After several hours of research, I became very tired and needed time to absorb the vast array of knowledge

I had received. I asked the assistant to escort me to my room so I could rest. So much had happened in the last few hours that I immediately fell asleep.

The Test of Survival

According to my watch, I had slept for several hours. When I awakened I felt a cool, relaxing air blowing over me that gave me the same feeling as having taken a tranquilizer pill. Immediately, I went back to sleep and began to dream. I could see myself approaching Atlantis in the undersea craft and being transferred to the main body of the city. The dream faded. It seemed so intoxicating that I felt soothed within and free of all reality surrounding me.

As I awakened, I felt very groggy and slowly sat up on the side of the bed. I looked around and was shocked to see that I was alone in what appeared to be a small bell tower sitting on the vast emptiness of the sea bottom secluded from the city.

Where am I? As I peered through the portholes, the city was nowhere in sight. *How can I be moved without any awareness?* It was almost like being anesthetized and never feeling it.

I realized I had to face facts. I was now in a new location and had to do something rational in the line of duty. Still, I was puzzled as to why I had been abandoned on such a lonely and far-out place. I noticed a green tint of light that evolved from a floor panel and gave off whimsical sounds of music or high operational frequency vibrations made to sound like music. With the sounds, I almost felt as if I were in a state of bewilderment.

Located on one side of the room was a door, and I wondered where it led. I didn't feel comfortable opening it and going out on my own because I thought the entire room would be flooded and I would drown. My phobia of the room began to close in on me. As I looked out the porthole, a strange vessel was approaching a large underground cavern of some sort. The cavern appeared to get larger. Eventually, the craft entered and then quickly disappeared.

Suddenly, I felt hope that I might escape this dungeon of fear. I walked back to my bed, sat down, and began to retrace all that had happened in the last hour. Maybe, if I could put the pieces together, I could gradually overcome my fears and escape. Plagued as I was by the small space inside the room, I could move about comfortably.

I remembered that when I awakened, I was still very sleepy. Obviously, I had been drugged and moved for some reason. What was I not supposed to see that might play a major role in my escape?

Strange as it was, I could still see myself being faced with impossible obstacles and miraculously escaping dangerous situations. I walked over to the window, looked out at the surrounding sea, and noticed it had blackened in color. *Obviously, it is nighttime.* The body of water was so dark and viscous that it seemed impenetrable in all its hue. The color of black was so dramatic that it took on aesthetic qualities.

This frightened me, and I moved away from the porthole and gazed at the wall where there was an indentation in the formation of a "V." What its function was, I could not tell at that point. My eyes seemed to focus on the V, and my head began to tingle as I fell helplessly to the floor.

I awakened quickly, and, to my surprise, I had once again been moved and was now lying somewhere on a beach. I was relieved to know that I was not locked in a room. I ran my hands across my body, and it felt warm and dry to the touch. To my knowledge, I had no physical abrasions or changes in my skin, only sand on my shoes and clothing. I probably looked as if I had struggled to shore under my own power and somehow made it safely.

I could feel the soothing, cool air as it seemed to glide over my body and gave me a feeling of relief, something I had not experienced for a long time. I stood up and stretched my arms. How good it felt to be free again! How was I to know what situations I still had to endure?

As I looked around, I thought, *where is the estate of Cantor?* All I could see was land and a vast area of woods, so I started walking away from the beach. Somehow, in this faraway place, I felt more at home in the natural habitat. It had been several years since I had visited a wooded area, so I just roamed aimlessly through the glen. I walked about two miles and decided to rest. Up to this point, I had not seen running water, although the environment was similar to an earthly forest. I had almost forgotten my bodily needs for food, and my hunger pains increased.

Thus far, I had scarcely noticed edible vegetation, but my appetite was becoming more real to me. Looking around, I spotted something resembling a fruit tree. I plucked two fruits from the branches and consumed them. After eating, I felt completely nourished. This was quite a change for me, as my food consumption for the last twelve years while in Galaxy Fourteen had mostly been provided through a form of energy capsules.

As I continued slowly walking through the glen, I realized I had consumed too much food in too short a time and lay down to rest. I wondered how long it would be before I had an opportunity such as this again. For once in my life, I dreamed fantasies of love, war, and recreational entities. I felt relaxed and free with the tension leaving my body.

$$\infty$$

I awakened shortly thereafter to discover the wooded glen was no longer visible. Seemingly, I had been moved again, and my perceptive abilities had been blocked. I was apparently locked into some long-range converter ray, which was connected to me and programmed to experience all these happenings.

The area was a most unusual setting this time, comparable to an arctic atmosphere of the twentieth century. I was even dressed in warm clothes to retain my body heat. Somehow, I had to pretend outwardly that the environment to which I was being subjected did not matter, and I had to interject myself into the forum as soon as possible.

At this point, I realized the need for making a decision. If I played the part intended for me, somehow everything would work out. Once again I found myself alone, and I cautiously walked over the barren tundra and under the polar ice cap with only one thought in mind—escape! The light source, probably a star, was just over the horizon, and the cold was piercing to my flesh. My need for warmth seemed too vast for words.

Even though I had sufficient clothing for the frigid climate, I was becoming worried over my bodily needs. Food was nowhere to be found, and I longed for help. *Please! Just anyone, help me!* This just couldn't be happening to me.

I found myself becoming aggressive in my thought-wave pattern and suddenly, almost traumatically, my environment seemed to swallow me as I sank into a deep, dark world of drowsiness.

Had I been overtaken by wild animals, killed and eaten, or attacked by unknown aliens of another world? I felt I could take whatever was happening to me mentally, physically, or emotionally, but there were no words to express why I, Kit Bartusch, a space engineer for the National Space Agency, had no control over what was happening to me.

Time passed quickly as I slept, awakened, and slowly opened my eyes. Looking over me was Lambda

Photon. Yes, out of all that had happened to me, I was back under the sea in the city of Atlantis—cold and hungry yet safe.

As my body shivered, Lambda Photon applied a warm heat ray that massaged my skin, restoring my body temperature. I knew this had to be real, as I could feel her hands touching me above my eyes and slowly pressing on my forehead. As she applied pressure, she activated the heat ray gun, and my appetite and cold were gone instantaneously.

What a homecoming for all I had experienced.

"Kit, to become a member of the order of the New Empire, a person must pass the test of the four torture planets and you passed rather easily. Your body has adapted well to space exploration in semi-evolved solar systems."

"I don't understand. Lambda Photon, why did I have to take such excruciatingly painful tests just to become a member of the New Empire? I thought your family had already accepted me without any further questions even though my point of origin was millions of miles away."

"Kit, the information I will next relate to you will not make you happy; however, you must be told the truth."

"What is it, Lambda Photon?"

"You can never transcend the time barrier and return to your home in Galaxy Fourteen."

I wondered what possibly could have happened that would leave me marooned here forever. *Am I destined to become a member of the thirty-second century, knowing I can never leave?*

"Lambda Photon, are you sure that I can't return to my own time in Galaxy Fourteen?"

"No, Kit."

"Then explain to me how your family is able to return to the estate of your father where I first encountered you when I departed the space hop?"

"Kit, I'll tell you the reason in the morning. You need rest. Now go to bed and get some sleep."

I felt both tired and sleepy, an experience that was intoxicating as well as soothing to my body. For once, I rested peacefully.

Alien Attack

All at once Lambda Photon rushed into my room and said, "Kit, I have some alarming news for you. I don't know what happened, but the shuttle craft in which you landed has returned to the spaceship, blasted off and mysteriously disappeared."

"Oh, no! How could that have happened? They would not leave me."

As sympathetic as she could possibly be, Lambda Photon told me she surmised that my people assumed I was dead and decided to leave.

Unbelievable! They will always wait for me, I thought to myself.

"Have your technologists tried to contact the spaceship?" I asked.

"Yes, the communications officer at central control tried to verify the spacecraft's trajectory and surmised that due to a large comet crossing its path, it had disintegrated."

"Thank you, Lambda Photon, for providing this information for me, but I just need to be alone for a while so I may reflect on everything I've just learned." Feeling deserted and upset, I knew I had to come to terms with what Lambda Photon told me.

Based on the new information I had just received, there would be no point in my making any attempts to return to Galaxy Fourteen. *In a way, it seems Lambda Photon is being truthful. Maybe she really does care for me.*

How difficult it was for me to accept the fact that my best friend, Steve Matthews, and all the other technicians and scientists with whom I had lived had been vaporized by a comet. *Is it possible for God to let this happen?* As I sat there all alone, the four walls seemed to be closing in on me. I decided to leave the building and began walking through the city. My heart was heavy, and my mind couldn't accept the fact that I was totally alone. *What can I do now but continue to put my trust in God?*

I thought for a moment about just how careless the *Fanfare* had been. But now I must live for the future, for I had become part of a new environment yearning for knowledge of the past, present, and future. I knew I needed to get in contact with Lambda Photon, as she would be worried about me. Still, I needed more time alone and didn't feel as if I could face anyone at present. Leaving my room, I eventually made my way to a museum, where it would be quiet, and I could grieve for the crew I so dearly loved.

The building was very similar to early renaissance architecture and had gorgeous spires that stood above it. The museum was not an intricate color of gold, but gray and black, laced with colors of red, green, and yellow. The colors were spectacular and seemed inviting. Finding the room vacant, I discovered pictures of the early people, armaments used in combat, and medicinal drugs used to fight diseases.

How scientific and culturally enriched these people seemed to be. Funny though, as I looked at the pictures, I seemed somewhat emotional and felt a sincere moment of true relief. The pictures revealed early Roman architecture and cultural designs typical of that era of time on Earth as was recorded by historians. Many of their early manuscripts were obviously translated from Sumerian to Latin by devout priests. Although these people were of another age and time, I guess they could still be referred to as ancient.

Strangely enough, the pictures were multicolored, somewhat an invention not introduced in our own time, but similar to the fifteenth or sixteenth century. Also, frames of gold design, carved out of what appeared to be wood, surrounded all the pictures.

Another object that I noticed was a tablet used to study seasons or possibly astrology. In early times, I knew that astrology forecasted the destiny of one's life for eternity. Also written on the tablets were predictions up to one thousand years in advance of the present society, and people had to follow them religiously.

It was not until the populace of Atlantis changed culturally and scientifically that they resolved themselves to a higher deity called God. Up to this point in time, astrology had provided the floor plan for life, and people believed this wholeheartedly without any questions.

Now the New Empire was strong and powerful. Their form of government had changed hands from an emperor to that of an aristocrat. Cantor and his family were in complete control of the government, and the people obeyed without question.

I left the museum and slowly walked down the street. I recalled that people navigated by means of a moving platform mounted beside the buildings. There weren't many people, although a few were visible to me. I thought this to be very unusual. The people must be somewhere besides in the city, perhaps secluded in a mining or building site. I also wondered about the disappearance of the undersea ship that I had seen. All this left me very perplexed, and I had numerous questions that needed answers.

Little did I know that my wait would be a short one. For some unexplainable reason, I got on the moving platform in front of a rather large building with windows but no entrance and moved steadily through the city.

It seemed like several minutes went by before I got off the platform and walked over to a fountain that resembled a large eagle. Jets of water sprayed from its wings and beak. I suppose that the eagle represented the strength of Atlantis, just as the eagle represented the strength of home. I looked at it for a moment and then turned around and noticed the large structure was protected by a dome.

Sometime later I realized I had traveled quite a distance through the city and must be exactly opposite from where I originally started. I walked over to a building with a sign that read, "All personnel beyond this gate require a pass from the Consul of Atlantis. All others keep out."

I also noticed that the building was heavily fortified and well protected. One man appeared, and before he entered, he was required to stand on a yellow platform in front of the structure as a dense, yellow light was aimed directly at him. The light ray seemed to permeate his entire body. I almost thought the man would cry out with raptures of pain or completely and undeniably change shape. Instead, as the light stopped, the man's clothing turned a bright yellow instead of a silver sheen, appearing as if the color were baked on. Immediately he got off the platform and walked into the building.

Up to this point, I felt as if I had freedom within the city; however, I needed to know if it were possible for me to get inside the mysterious building.

Thus reconciled to my dilemma, I returned to the building of Cantor's domain in the underwater city. It seemed to take about seventeen minutes on the moving platform. Strange as it seems, there were people, both men and women, moving to and fro, hardly noticing my presence.

I got off the platform and immediately noticed an aroma of hot bread baking. Going inside the building, I saw others eating, so I asked for a piece of bread, and it was given to me freely with no monetary exchange. In many respects, this type of life favored a commune, similar to that of an early socialist regime, yet unified in its entirety.

I then got back on the platform and proceeded on my journey. As I moved along, I noticed that the faces of the people showed little expression, whether it be sympathy or joy, toward one another.

Shortly thereafter, I arrived at the embarkation terminal. I was still suspicious of everyone, including Lambda

Photon. As I walked in, I was greeted by a messenger beckoning me to follow him. Instead of moving slowly down the corridor, a part of the wall moved back, and we literally ran down a long, narrow hallway. Suddenly, the courier stopped, pressed a lever on the wall, and directly in front of me was an undersea craft.

We boarded the craft, and it started rising immediately, taking approximately ten seconds. After reaching the surface, we were teleported back to Cantor's palace. From what I gathered, a major crisis had occurred, and the New Empire was being threatened by an alien attack. For once, I was scared and more than willing to use my knowledge to help in any way I could.

How could aliens attack such an impervious civilization, seemingly resistant to attack from any outside source? Somehow I knew my reactions had to be identical to others, as my life was also being threatened.

I asked, "Would someone go get Lambda Photon for me?" As the messenger left, I prayed silently to God to protect us from an attack. *I believe he is our only hope for survival at this point in time.*

"Kit, what is wrong?" asked Lambda Photon.

"I'm so unsure of what is going to happen to us."

"Maybe I can explain to you the situation in which we are currently involved. We have never actually seen the enemy but have received bits of flying debris aimed directly at our galaxy. We are protected by an array of cosmic energy in the form of solar plasma. It is similar to a force field that surrounds a planet and protects it from forms of infrared and ultraviolet radiation."

"That helps some, but I need to know if you are a God-fearing person."

"What in the world do you mean, Kit?"

"Do you not realize there is a God who created everything, including us? He loves and cares about us. He even forgives us when we sin and pray for forgiveness."

"Kit, our people worship many gods. To worship one God would not be feasible."

"Lambda Photon, my God is one God, the one and only God!"

Somehow I have to make her understand about God, as I know this will definitely be a turning point in our relationship.

"Lambda Photon, I need to know if you trust and love me enough that you will pray to my God and accept him as your Savior? He has legions of angels ready to help you. I can't fathom the idea of going through life without God's support and guidance. He will help both of us get through all conflicts we have to face in life."

"Let me think about all you have said, as everything about your God is new to me. Can you give me some time?"

"Yes, Lambda Photon, I can give you all the time you need."

"Kit, it is imperative that we put our conversation on hold and report to the defense area right away."

"Just lead the way," I said.

I didn't know what to expect and was surprised when we entered a type of land vehicle and moved swiftly to the area assigned for defense personnel. Soon we entered a technologically equipped room that monitored the movement of space machines throughout the New Empire. In many respects, the area looked almost the same as a rocket propulsion control room for in-depth observatory studies. At the end of the room, flights from planet to planet, as well as potential invaders, could be monitored.

At that time, the flying debris was being pulverized by the solar plasma, and bits of rock were moving back in the opposite direction. Actually, there seemed to be no imminent danger. However, I did learn that wherever one is, at home or in an unknown environment, there is always fear of the enemy.

Lambda Photon and I returned to our space-monitored vehicle and went hurriedly to the underground city. As we traveled back, I suppose I began to daydream. I thought of the marvel ray and its many uses. Since I had been here, to my knowledge, Cantor had made no use of it. I needed to ask if I would be permitted to project it back to my own galaxy.

"Kit, quit daydreaming and thinking about your home in Galaxy Fourteen."

I wondered how she always knew what I was thinking although I suspect she had the ability to read my mind as she constantly said things about what I was thinking.

"Kit, are you listening to me? Galaxy Fourteen is probably desolate, and the remains of a city or complex may only resemble an area in total disarray." *She simply can't understand how very disturbing this information is to me.*

My daydream ended as we arrived and left the craft. I realized many of my questions had been answered in a very short length of time.

I then went back to my assigned room for some much-needed rest and relaxation. Seemingly, I had escaped once again without any bodily harm. I walked in and found my room had not undergone any changes. For some reason, I instinctively looked at my watch and noticed that it was three in the afternoon.

As I scanned the horizon from the terrace, the sunlight made it look as if tiny fireballs were moving the hour and minute hands on my watch. It must have been only a reflection of the sunlight.

I turned on my communicator and tried again to make contact with the space hop. Still, no answer. *Lambda Photon must be telling me the truth.*

I sat down on my bed and began to piece the parts of this great jigsaw puzzle together. Almost at once, I drew a blank at formidable explanations. Perhaps my movements were monitored and timing was essential to my well-being in places as well as in space. The only changes that seemed to occur to me could be attributed to time travel—the up-and-down movements through the underground cavern to the surface and back. Knowing I could do nothing, I then lay down to sleep, as my mind had undergone strenuous changes, and the sleep was soothing to the inner workings of my brain and consciousness.

Trust versus Distrust

After a while, I awakened to feel cool air flowing over my body in an undulating movement. I quickly recognized this air as the same type that had directed me to the four torture planets. Only this time, I got up and escaped. No telling what had been planned for me in terms of change. I had meandered from one locale to another, only to be re-united with these aliens.

I gazed over the terrace of the countryside and once again began to think in terms of escape. *What could happen if I make an attempt to leave? Would I be recaptured and brought back to this so-called dungeon of fear?*

Perhaps this was only an afterthought, but it truly plagued me, and there seemed no way to rid these thoughts from my mind. Among many of the issues that intimidated me, the most important factor was escape, which seemed unlikely for the moment.

I decided to return to the alien library to observe the memory banks once again. I had already heard the tapes, but there were many questions yet unanswered in my mind. I walked into the library only to face other aliens listening to tapes or records. Nothing was alphabetized since man had begun using computers instead of the universal number system of the last one thousand years.

Why at this moment did I begin to think of the past? Could I have lived before? Was there a facet of my life yet unknown to me? I began thinking about my early childhood years. I vaguely remembered things I did when I was about seven years old, but earlier than that was a blank. I knew when I was young I was with my parents, who loved me very much, and then for some reason, we got separated. At that time, I was put in a children's ward and taken care of by some adults.

As the years passed, I never lost my faith in God, even when separated from my parents. My only realization was that they must have been shielding me from something bad. What it could have been, I didn't know.

Before leaving on this mission, I had been checked thoroughly in medical and space experimentation and was basically sound in every way. I then began to wonder. *Am I returning home? If so, where is home?*

An earthly module was all I had ever known in Galaxy Fourteen. My physical, mental, and psychological appearance seemed to be similar to everyone else. I began to question my validity as a human being. Was I really a piece of inanimate matter experimentally derived from a test tube in a scientist's laboratory? Who were my parents? Where did I live? Where did my formal education begin? I seemed to be an intellectual person.

I worried over these questions with spontaneous confusion and bewilderment. I had much to learn, and my enthusiasm was greatly accelerated. I pulled out a tape from the memory bank, which was labeled *48957404a*. There were numerous other tapes, but for some unexplainable reason, I selected this one.

The tape explained the journey from the ill-fated city of Atlantis on the Earth to its present location. The manner in which travel was permitted by the saucer seemed very sophisticated, even if this took place four-to-five-thousand years ago. There seemed to be all kinds of indistinguishable sounds in the background as it played, yet something sounded vaguely familiar.

The information was like a storybook of some sort or a delusion of intangible perspectives. As the story unfolded, meetings with alien spaceships from other galaxies and attacks from flying debris constantly causing repairs aboard the spacecraft were revealed.

All the way through the recorded message there was a central voice that seemed to echo in my mind as if it were someone very dear to me. *Am I on board this spaceship as a suspended life form in a scientist's laboratory?*

Still unsatisfied, I pulled another tape that instantly released a loud, humming alarm. What had I done to cause these events? The librarian rushed over to me and said in a thunderous voice, "Eject that disk from the computer at once! Do it now!"

Frightened to death, I did as she demanded and the alarm stopped. *What did I do wrong?*

Lambda Photon rushed over to me and very quietly instructed me to leave with her and I was to ask no questions as we were leaving.

I felt like an intruder as we left. What was now in store for me? Was I to be extinguished from life as I knew it? The future of my life lay before me like the sunset of Galaxy Fourteen. Lambda Photon ushered me back to my room and said, "Kit, you just need time to rest and reflect on everything you have learned in such a short period of time."

"Lambda Photon, I'm very fond of you."

"Kit, I need for you to stop worrying and just enjoy being with me. I have problems of my own that scare me. I need both of us to be strong when I share these problems with you. Be patient and trust me."

Placing her hand on my shoulder, she hugged me and tried to reassure me that I would get through the ordeal and to never forget that she loved me very much. "Kit, I will return for you in a little while after talking with my mother."

Click went the lock on the door. I wondered, *Why am I being locked in my room again?*

Immediately, I noticed something different about the room. There were now various pictures of families hanging on the walls. I felt as though I was in someone's bedroom, yet, inconceivably, all tension from the previous routine flushed from my body.

I walked over to my bed and lay down. Almost at once, it was as if I had fallen asleep; yet somehow I was aware of everything around me. The sleep relaxed my body, and I felt a tingling sensation once more, as though my soul were leaving my body.

The sleeplessness wasn't linked with my brain, for I sensed little as far as the reality of existence. Actually, I was afraid to sleep. Fear seemed to grasp my life, and for some unknown reason, my autonomic nervous system was in a panic, leaving me somewhere out of the mainstream of life.

A few hours passed in the wake of this phenomenon. It felt as if I were watching a monitored playback of my autobiography. I began to worry about life and death.

Probably my mind was fantasizing, and I toyed with the idea of being a highly skilled life-like robot programmed to experience all the activities of an actual human being, even to the point of identifying the race of man. Could I be sure, or was this another disillusion of childlike make-believe?

Somehow my subconscious mind regained the strength of sleep, and I seemed to pass over the twilight of darkness. Even though I had been aroused by the very inkling of thought transmission on a highly specialized form, my brain allowed sleep and peace.

The Rejection

I awakened suddenly with a headache in my temples. Instead of waiting for Lambda Photon to come get me, I tried the door and found it unlocked. I decided to go to the hospital for a medical checkup. When I entered the hospital, I went directly to the blood department and asked for a blood test. My papers were carefully examined and processed in a microcomputer that spoke in a human-like voice, "Patient unacceptable at this time." The message both shocked and insulted me. I asked to be tested for anemia and was politely refused. But why should I be refused? Others who were there were receiving medical checkups.

Perhaps the only difference lay in the color of my skin; mine being white and theirs olive. In my opinion, this was discrimination at its worst. Racial problems of this type had been overcome nearly one thousand years ago by our descendants. In some respects, I felt as though I was toxic to the touch.

I left the hospital and stepped onto the platforms designed for travel throughout the city. The void in my mind was rapidly becoming filled with knowledge, and I sensed relief in spite of all that had happened in the last hour.

I returned to the quarters provided me and began an unusual interrogation of myself. Fear had never seemed obvious despite what might happen to me in this unique physical state.

I felt my subconscious drift on higher levels of emotional frequencies; however, I still had questions and periods of uncertainty. I knew that with the help of the most brilliant scientists, chaos can still plague the human mind in its search for uninterrupted knowledge of the sciences and arts.

I was not the type who gave up on any endeavor. Neither apathy nor temporal thoughts were on my mind as I gazed around the room. I felt a strong impulse permeating my entire being, letting me know that all was well. The impulse seemed to radiate above my eyes, and at times I wondered if this was the beginning of a modular headache.

I tried not to let my failures perplex me just because I could not be tested at the hospital. For some unexplainable reason, I got up from a sitting position, walked around the room, and began to observe ornaments, pictures, and wall decorations. They were multicolored and resembled people I had observed on the moving platform during my recent exploration of the city.

My thoughts were transfixed on a particular person in one of the pictures. I immediately recognized the man as the same one who had entered the building earlier. A yellow light had seemed to permeate his entire body for a few seconds, and he then entered the building. *What can he possibly be doing?*

All at once, I felt a desire to pull myself together, leave the module, and go directly to the restricted area. I realized I might be followed, so I left calmly, but with one idea in mind—*Find out what is in the restricted area.*

I knew I needed a pass from the Consul of Atlantis before I could enter the mysterious building, so I stopped at Lambda Photon's module.

Upon arriving, I felt a reverberation directly over my eyes, hurting for a few seconds, and then ceasing. I pressed the lever on her module, and a light was beamed directly at me. Then the door opened, and I entered. I expected Lambda Photon would be there to meet me; however, she was not.

I heard a computerized voice say, "Kit, are you there?"

I recognized the voice to be that of Lambda Photon, so I answered, "Yes, I'm waiting on you. Where are you?"

"Sit tight, I'll be there in two Earth minutes."

I wondered, *How did her computerized voice machine know it was me?*

I then surmised the light that was aimed at me must have had a built-in television camera with memory. I seemed to have little to worry about as I walked around her module. I really had romantic feelings for Lambda Photon in some unexplainable way; therefore, I didn't anticipate any surprises. I knew it wasn't infatuation, because every time I was with her, there seemed to always be something wonderful and loving about her attitude and interest in me.

I now realized that she was the key to my success in obtaining the pass. I wanted desperately to fulfill my curiosity about this city and its people in the days ahead. It seemed as if seconds passed as I looked around her module. I even sneaked a look in her closet and found some bright metallic clothing. One of the drawers in her chest had a small, pocket-sized machine with one switch and a yellow light on it. My brain immediately sent impulses like the speed of light to detect its usefulness.

I wondered if this was the key to entering the restricted building. As I picked up the strange mechanical device and observed it, I sensed the presence of someone else in the room with me.

Atomic Fortress

I turned around instantaneously to find Lambda Photon staring at me as I held the object in my hand. She knew that my curiosity had led to meddling with things I shouldn't have, but she acted as though everything was okay.

She asked, "Did you find what you were looking for?"

I said, "Yes, I believe so."

"Lambda Photon, can I borrow this object for a little while and return it later today?"

"Sure, Kit. You have my permission to study the instrument. However, you do need to be careful which button you push as each one has multiple functions."

She walked toward me and placed both of her soft, feminine hands on my forehead just above my eyes. They felt like warm sunlight touching the brow of nature's realm. Her eyes were fixed on mine in a warm and tranquil way.

At once she read my inner thoughts. Momentarily, she smiled. Removing her hands from my forehead, she then placed her hand on mine and led me over to one of the space relaxers built to seat two people comfortably.

We sat down and faced each other. She immediately said, "What are your intentions?"

For some reason, I knew she was going to say that.

I replied, "I've traveled all over the universe, seen many great and unbelievable things, feared for my life, and escaped harmful situations, but never before have I had the pleasure of being with such a charming, beautiful woman."

She knew that I was sincere and listened with love in her heart. I took her hands in mine and embraced her.

"Kit, I love you so much. My life would not be the same without you. If I should ever call you, will you come to me?"

Is she trying to warn me about something?

I replied, "Yes, I will always be here for you."

Lambda Photon got up from the space relaxer and walked over to the door of her module. She appeared nervous, and I knew she needed reassurance.

"Kit, first of all, let me say that I dearly love you, but I need to discuss with you the causes of my fear. My family likes you. However, they have made it very clear if we continue our relationship and eventually marry, I will be banished from our civilization, and my body will be deprogrammed and sterilized in the medical units, thus preventing me from ever having children. I feel it would be unfair to you if I did not tell you the truth. I also want you to know that each time I leave you I am required to report to my parents before returning to my module. I have been forced to follow their rules."

"Lambda Photon, I'm falling in love with you. I never realized the pressure you have been under and the major decisions with which you are faced."

"Kit, my heart is reaching out to you, although my fears are real."

"Lambda Photon, you must now trust me to help get us through this ordeal. We will find a solution, even if we have to travel into time. Don't mention this to anyone, even your most trusted servant."

I knew time was of the essence, and we needed to proceed with our work. "Lambda Photon, what's inside the restricted area?"

"Kit, if you really want to know, take my hand and follow along beside me. Be sure to keep the scientific instrument in your other hand."

Also, she placed a V-shaped pin on my clothing that glowed brightly. We left her module and got on one of the moving platforms. Like lovers, we gazed at the sights of the city with smiles on our faces and love in our hearts.

Although my love for Lambda Photon was obvious, I still needed to see inside the restricted building. I sincerely felt it was the key to my survival. The restricted area was rapidly coming into view, and my heart began to pound. My nerve impulses felt like butterflies fluttering to and fro.

Soon the restricted area was in full view, and Lambda Photon and I departed the moving platform and walked toward the building. "Kit, I need you to follow my instructions. Turn the lever to the right on the machine, and a yellow light should illuminate."

We walked to a platform, and a translucent yellow light beam penetrated our bodies from head to toe. Each of us turned a golden color that gleamed brightly. We entered the building and were instructed by automatic wall monitors to follow the arrows to a large fortified door.

The entrance resembled that of a large cave. A computer voice then instructed us to turn off the mechanical device I held in my hand. As I did so, the entrance door opened slowly, revealing a cave with many catacombs and phosphorescent rocks.

Lambda Photon and I walked forward. Truthfully, I was afraid, but her willingness to continue eased my consciousness. We walked up and down corridors that were wide enough for at least six men to walk side by side. The ceiling stood about twelve feet in height.

We walked about a mile, and I began to feel tired. Lambda Photon suggested I stop and rest for a couple of minutes. She pressed on her V-shaped pin. Suddenly a place in the rock opened, and a portable oxygen unit fell onto the cave floor and immediately began to inflate. "Kit, place the small mask over your nose and mouth and slowly breathe in the oxygen. I'll tell you when to stop. You have to put your trust in me."

"Okay, I'll do as you say." I felt so tired. *Why am I the only one who feels these symptoms?* After a few minutes, Lambda Photon removed the mask and laid it aside. I felt much better, and she once again motioned for me to follow her.

The surprise of my life was yet to come. We traveled another mile until we came to a gigantic room in the cave with what looked like a large, walled fortress located directly in the center of the room. It was approximately 300 by 600 feet. I stood there in awe for several minutes while looking at this massive underground fortress. The ceiling of the cave looked like it was perhaps 200 feet high and reflected light from its natural phosphorescence. The room glowed in intensity, as if it were electrically lighted.

Lambda Photon led me toward the walled fortress, which I had to touch in order to satisfy my curiosity that it was indeed real. The fortress was a dark gray color and looked very old. It could easily have passed for the biblical walls of Jericho on Earth thousands of years ago. The walls appeared to be 80 to 100 feet in height. Also, they resembled huge, granite rocks hewn together, weighing many tons, and lying in symmetrical layers stacked one on top of the other.

The fortress was a perfect rectangle with one large entrance. There were no other hidden entrances or exits that I could detect. However, this entrance looked as if it had a heavy iron door that was approximately 20 feet tall and 20 feet wide. There didn't appear to be any other human beings in the area as far as I could see.

I asked Lambda Photon, "What is this place?"

For a moment, she was silent. Then she replied, "This is the source of all life-giving power to the New Empire."

I felt this odd-looking place could not possibly have any supernatural or real power to create life forms that resembled people. In many ways, the old fortress was bizarre and rather scary.

I wanted to know the type of power needed to sustain life in the New Empire. After all, I had had some rather unbelievable things happen to me since I left the *Fanfare* for this journey through time.

Lambda Photon then said, "You will find it difficult to believe or understand what I am about to tell you. What you would have termed one hundred years or centuries in Galaxy Fourteen is but only an inkling of time here because of our accelerated time travel through space. The energy that we use to run all the power is derived from the core of smaller planets, housed inside this great fortress in suspended animation. The energy travels in a circular cylinder at a velocity slightly less than the speed of light.

"Certain planets in our galaxy are traveling so rapidly around their respective stars that from deep in space light coming away from that star system looks like one bright star rather than a star group consisting of many planets orbiting their respective stars. By obtaining the primordial heat from the core of less than light speed or Warp 1, this energy could last infinitesimally according to our needs in space for heat, electrical power, protection, and the creation of synthetic foods."

I was truly fascinated and at last felt a coolness I had not enjoyed in some time. At least there appeared to be something concrete in this heat expansion theory. The pure expansion of molecules of heat traveling slightly less than the speed of light was the scientific find of the universe.

I began to fantasize what we could have done with this power back in Galaxy Fourteen. Lambda Photon realized my confusion and amazement as she used her extrasensory perception skills to once again read my mind. "Kit, only skilled workers are permitted inside the fortress."

At this point I wondered if our lives were in danger. *With all the lead shielding used to protect us from the radioactivity being given off, I am unsure if I made the right decision in asking to be brought to this location.*

Lambda Photon looked reassuringly at me, and said, "We don't have anything to fear unless a crack develops in the wall. That is very unlikely to happen as the area was built as an earthquake-free zone, and the power source would have never been placed inside if it were not safe." With this information, I continued to wonder, *Did we make a mistake by entering the fortress?*

We walked around the fortress until we came to a screen that reflected light from the center. I could clearly see the workers behind shields, constantly checking the heat sources.

Never had I experienced anything so finite and meticulous. I was seeing living antimatter being harnessed and releasing abundant power.

"Kit, can you believe we are actually looking at atomic energy at work?"

I think she realizes I am speechless and find it hard to believe all the amazing technological advancements that are being made within the confines of this area.

We then left the fortress for our return trip back through the caverns. I was very excited and had many questions yet to be answered.

The Mystifying Cave

As we began our return trip, I experienced some type of feeling resembling a spasm in my head. It was like an atomic power pack being energized to the maximum threshold of endurance. I felt as if my brain would withdraw from my skull casing and become as one with inanimate matter that permeated this strange and unpredictable place. Even Lambda Photon exhibited concern at the pain I was experiencing.

I grabbed both sides of the temples of my head as if I had heard decibels of music at ultrasonic frequencies that were too shrill. The pain felt as if daggers were stabbing my head. I wanted to believe that the pain would stop; however, it was so intense that I had to close my eyes. Then, just as quickly as it began, the pain disappeared.

When I opened my eyes, I realized I was blind. I frantically reached for Lambda Photon. She sensed my need for help and took hold of me. Somehow I felt safe in her arms.

"Kit, do you think you have a severe headache? Or is something else wrong?"

"I'm not sure. Does anything about me look different?"

"Yes, your eyes are glowing a bright green."

"I can't see! Help me, Lambda Photon!"

"Kit, you must calm down and put these opaque goggles on. Don't be alarmed. Your sight will return.

Just hold onto me, and I'll guide your steps."

I did as I was instructed and stayed close to her, holding her hand as we walked out.

All sorts of strange thoughts escaped from the inner workings of my brain. I loved Lambda Photon, but I had never been in a situation such as this. Was I being taken to the end of my body's existence and transformed into a new human torso, fully equipped to surpass my former body form?

I walked with uncertainty as we left the power center and returned to the city.

"Kit, I realize we have been walking here for quite a while. Let's stop, and I'll guide you to sit down on the seat directly behind you. Do you feel okay now?"

"Yes, but will you still be with me?"

"Don't worry. I'm right beside you. I'm placing a seat belt over both our laps to secure us as we will be moving at a rapid speed on the monorail. Don't be afraid. I will not let anything happen to you."

At least this was better than walking, which was a new learning experience for me. Never before in my lifetime had anything like this happened to me.

I was using my sense of hearing as my sense of sight, like looking from the inside of my body outward toward everything around me measured in sound decibels familiar to previously transmitted knowledge I learned from youth. All the time that we were moving, I had these thoughts.

Was I supposed to think along categorical lines of thought or trauma, pre-diagnosed by the libido of the mind, or was this normal thought transmission for human beings? I found that I was doing some soul-searching because of my mysterious circumstances.

Abruptly, we came to a stop. I don't really understand how we moved, as I felt we had been sitting still for ten minutes. "Is everything okay, Lambda Photon? We've been sitting here for a good while, and you haven't said anything."

"Kit, I felt we needed time for your eyes to adjust to the changing light conditions after having been so near the restricted area. You may now remove the goggles."

Afterward she was astonished when she looked into my eyes. They were not flickering anymore; however, a bright hue of green color was still obvious. Strangely, I realized I could see. I wondered, *Will the blindness reoccur?* I pondered this thought for a few minutes as we walked back through the cave toward the city.

"Lambda Photon, could this happen to me again?

"Not likely, Kit. I've never seen anyone's eyes turn a bright green as if they had been dilated in some way."

"I was afraid to ask you, but I had to know. Did I frighten you, dear?"

"No, Kit. My only recourse was to weaken the light in your eyes using the goggles so that in time your eyes would return to normal."

I wondered, *Are my facial features mutated in any way? Perhaps Lambda Photon is no longer attracted to me.*

"Kit, quit thinking negative thoughts. I'm pledged to you for life, regardless of what happens to either of us."

Lambda Photon then continued to lead me onward. "We need to stop here, turn to the right, and begin walking downward. There is nothing to fear. We're safe now."

I sense she realizes how reassuring those words are to me.

We stopped and she reached up to a stone projecting from the wall. As she touched it with her index finger, a wall opened from nowhere. I was as intrigued by this place as Tom Sawyer and Huckleberry Finn must have been when exploring a ghostly and dark cave.

We walked into the area like mystic explorers opening the tomb of a pyramid and finding the wealth of the ancient pharaohs—conquerors of inner space itself. This time there were no banners waving or songs of happiness courting our steps as we journeyed through the delicate passageways.

Suddenly, we came to a halt and stopped at a solid wall which had ancient forms of writing on it, much like a rebus. I said to Lambda Photon, "Don't hurry. Let's stop and decipher some of the ancient history of what appeared to be a very intelligent and remarkable race of people."

I wondered if such a rebus could possibly have been the creation of a super-race yet unknown to me. I considered the educated stone knowledge I had received in my early training as a space engineer in extraterrestrial life and suddenly a thought-wave pattern seemed to print out in my mind—the recapitulation theory, or doctrine of man. Could this only be an attempt to rationalize the idea that when the rebus was created on the stone face of the wall, man was only sub-par in intelligence and embodied and often bewailed the concept of pantheism as a guide for life on this planet?

Lambda Photon more or less laughed at me in deference to my affluent wisdom at reading the strange message. She asked, "Aren't you ready to go and see what else there is?"

"You would like for me to quit and leave, wouldn't you?"

She jokingly made fun of me and tugged at my hand to follow her.

"I am intrigued by the message, as it must relate to the inscriptions from a scientific point of view," I replied.

"Now, Kit, don't get caught up with these silly statements. I know there must be more to the actual translation than we can decipher from mere words."

Actually, the rebus was quite funny in a poem, which at the time of reading seemed incomprehensible. I knew there had to be more meaning here than a child's mimicry of a fable learned at a young age. The rebus inscription emitted phosphorescent light which meant that it must be important.

The rebus read as follows: "Mary very easily makes jam; she uses nice plums." Looking at the inscription, even a space scientist would have had a big laugh.

Finally, Lambda Photon tugged on my arm and encouraged me to leave. For some unaccountable reason, those translated words seemed to echo in my mind, just as a computer tape echoes in a microcosm of mechanical gibberish.

Once again Lambda Photon touched a stone that projected above my right shoulder. Instantly the stone wall moved, and my fondness of the place seemed to dissipate as we entered a large room filled with skilled technicians who were constantly at work. Could they be doctors? Surgical technicians? Mechanical engineers? Or was this recycled space debris made to mimic scientists at work?

Whatever or whomever these people were, they wore bright, white clothing covering the entire body except for eye slots and what looked like a place beneath the eyes for speaking. How they breathed was a mystery.

As we walked through the stone portals onto a wire mesh floor panel, a bright light aimed from the ceiling passed through us, lasting perhaps ten seconds. Then it stopped. One of the white-uniformed technicians motioned for us to follow him. We walked around the large room which was divided and subdivided like a giant beehive, except it was all on one level.

Lots of white-uniformed people worked in each cavity, which resembled small booths. Even though Lambda Photon and I walked by these unusual people, they seemed unconcerned with our presence and went about their work. I noticed that Lambda Photon showed little expression as we walked and seemed content that I follow her and ask no questions.

The room was illuminated with very bright light. We walked for about two or three minutes, and then the attendant motioned me to stop in front of a white portal resembling an operating table with four attendants around it and a bright light suspended from the ceiling. Also, there were all sorts of mechanical devices sitting on each side of the table that looked like they were used to tune up or refurbish a flying saucer.

One of the white-uniformed attendants motioned me to come forward and lie down on the table. Frankly, I was reluctant to do so. Lambda Photon once again seemed to come to my rescue.

"Kit, do you remember what happened to your eyes?"

"Well, of course I do. That was a very frightening experience."

"Then, all you need to do is lie down on the examination table so they can scan your eyes to detect for an overdose of radiation."

I realized the importance of the detection for radiation, but I wasn't too sure that I wanted strangers to check my body. I reluctantly lay down, and one of the attendants immediately placed both his hands on my shoulders and pressed downward as if he wanted me to lie still for a moment. An instrument of some sort, shaped like a black box with green, red, and blue lights that emanated from the outside, was projected over my body.

Next, some type of helmet was placed over my head and neck with a glass shield to protect me from the scanning rays. It was also apparent these people were very concerned about the intake of foreign matter into their bodies, whether it was infrared or ultraviolet radiation or microbes of an unknown origin.

Some type of jelly substance was then sprayed over the entire surface of my body. It felt sticky on the exposed part of my clothing where my skin penetrated the knitted material. Still, I was afraid to move. Call it fear, superstition, or hysteria. Whatever was happening almost anesthetized me into hallucinations. I even fantasized myself as a monster from the deep sea in this gel-type makeup. The substance remained on my body for about ten minutes.

Then the black box was removed, and a type of spray hose came out of one of the machines. Immediately, a yellow powder was then sprayed all over me. As it stopped, an attendant removed the helmet from my head and neck with the finesse of a skilled surgeon. I felt like I was still lost in the myriad of inner space. Then the same attendant who had pressed my shoulders down pulled them slowly upward until I was in a sitting position.

I looked down at my clothing and hands. Strangely, everything appeared the same as when I had come into this place. I knew I seemed very confused and disoriented.

My desire was to ask the uniformed attendants about all the tests that had just been performed; however, I felt this wasn't the place to question her in spite of the circumstances surrounding the strange incident.

I got off the table, and she took my hand and tugged with a strange force, almost that of escape. We walked twenty-five feet away from the booth toward a sliding door in the wall. I needed to find out exactly what was going on, but I didn't want to give the appearance that I was suspicious and overly curious. Someone might get the wrong impression, and I knew that ideas could quickly blow out of proportion.

I couldn't afford to lose my close relationship with Lambda Photon and her family as they were the key to my survival. Lambda Photon had pledged her life to me, and I knew if I damaged my only connection with her, I would be in trouble. With little hesitation, I then followed her to the moving doors.

"Kit, we need to wait for a moment. Please be patient." She took her hand and placed it on my cheek in a loving way and pressed gently. Then she withdrew her hand, and the doors opened automatically. "Follow me and stay close to my side," she said.

We walked through the moving doors and entered another segment of the cave which was well lit because of its phosphorescent rock. I walked a few steps and turned around to look behind me. Shock seemed to permeate my total being at what I saw. There were not any doors in sight, and all I could see was solid rock. Maybe I really did have radiation poisoning or was on a hallucinogenic trip in a microcosm of inner space.

"Kit, you need to catch up with me. We can't remain idle even for a few minutes."

"Why the concern, dear?"

"You don't understand. Within these confines there are surveillance cameras with monitors that record every few seconds the movements that are made. This enables them to keep the areas safe. We will be allowed a reasonable time for our exploration. However, if we stay too long, security will show up and escort us out of the cave. Do you understand?"

"Yes, I know all about surveillance techniques."

Trusting Lambda Photon

We walked along a rocky corridor for a few minutes, but I stopped for a moment to look at some pictures. These walls had ancient colored pictures similar to caveman illustrations of early animals. Most, however, were faded and one could easily understand the obvious change throughout the epochs of time. Again, Lambda Photon called for me to catch up with her. I was intrigued with the ancient pictures and hieroglyphs that were adjacent to my sides as I walked onward.

I guess I looked like a little boy in a big toy store, full of things with which to play. Somehow I was able to catch up with Lambda Photon. She stood there as if she had been waiting all her life for me. She changed her facial expressions as she looked at me. Whether she was upset or bored was of little concern to me at the moment.

I began to feel a reverberation of a high-pitched sound in my left ear, which quickly spread to the inner workings of my brain. The pain seemed to grasp me as if in complete control, and I was just an inanimate object programmed to perform certain autonomic activities of a real life human being.

The pain continued for perhaps ten seconds and then lapsed. Then, oh, no! The pain was starting again.

"At this moment, we can't worry about your pain. Keep up with me, Kit. Ultrasonic waves from the alarms may be interfering with your eyes or your brain waves. Don't worry. The pain will eventually cease."

My patience was growing thin with the pain, and I felt as if she should be more concerned; however, she lacked all emotion this time.

I grabbed hold of her and turned her to face me. I was upset because of her lack of concern for me. I looked at those wary and calculating eyes. She began interrogating my thoughts as a computer would dissect the internal parts of a combustion engine about to be dismounted for inspection.

"Kit, stand still! I'm going to place my hands over your eyes for one minute. When I remove my hands, we will continue walking in the cave."

"Will the alarm sound if we stand here for a minute?"

"No, Kit. I'm just being cautious with your eyes."

Nothing really seemed to happen physically that I could detect.

Once again we walked up to a wall that seemed to be the end of the cave. She then placed her hand on the protruding piece of rock that jetted outward, and the front wall moved to the left.

For some unexplainable reason, I was reluctant to continue with her. She jerked my hand to follow her, but I immediately pulled my hand back. She gave a sigh of distaste at my surprise move. Reluctantly, I clasped her hand and held it firmly.

"Lambda Photon, listen to me. Explain why we have to ascend to the city in this fashion. I'm getting tired of all the surprise passageways we have to go through. Can't we return a shorter way to the surface of the city?"

Lambda Photon replied, "Each portal that we have passed through has its own built-in sound decibel level that protects and insulates the upper level of the city from shock waves in the form of linear or longitudinal waves of seismic origin."

If I had even thought about earthquakes happening, I might not have entered these intricate catacombs. I began to think back to the early experimental studies I had undergone in Galaxy Fourteen concerning the study of thermodynamics using alpha particle analysis as a method of insulation.

This was the ultimate use of man's knowledge put to the test. The Atlanteans had taken a fragment of nuclear energy and harnessed its amazing properties. The entire shell of the cave was protected by sound vibrations, which were dissected at different ground levels, metered from Cantor's defense area.

Lambda Photon began interrogations of my mind and then smiled, which was a surprise to me. She took my hand and led me into the next room that was made up of what appeared to be rocks. Again there were pictures on the wall. I expected to see cavemen pictures or animal drawings. Instead, there were maps with ancient cities labeled on them.

At once, Lambda Photon read my mind and told me that the early Atlanteans had full knowledge of the whereabouts of these ancient cities. They used their flying columns to move close, make their design, and leave unnoticed by any people along the

Mediterranean Sea.

The early Macedonians would have only thought their gods were unhappy with them if they had seen something flying over their homeland with people aboard. So to avoid distasteful circumstances with the different races of man, the Atlanteans were able to observe the different people at work, at war, during migration to new lands, as well as the growth of nations.

The mere fact that the city of Atlantis even existed was sheer fantasy to the people along the Mediterranean Sea. The people of Atlantis were adamant that the outside world should know nothing of their existence. After all, their people were far more intellectually gifted in the hierarchy of man.

The people and colonies of Atlantis had a higher culture, economy, technology, and communication that surpassed even the most advanced civilization of the eastern part of the known world.

It would be five thousand years later before these nations along the Mediterranean Sea achieved the early status of the Atlanteans.

How calm and quiet I felt at the realization of something so lifelike yet familiar. We continued our walk until we came to a large, flat rock located directly to our left. There were two push buttons on the side of the rock. Lambda Photon walked over and touched a button on the right. In a few seconds, the surface of the rock looked like an illuminated television set. She then pressed the button on the bottom left of the screen and one of the early flights from the city of Atlantis to Eastern Europe and the Mediterranean Sea was taking place.

I realized this was a filmed sequence of what took place on one of the flying columns. We could see the design of the early cities, the dress code of the people, types of war and violence, modes of travel by the use of animals, ships, and the wheel, which I thought was nonexistent for many centuries. To avoid being seen in the skies, the Atlanteans made the outside of their flying columns glow as if they were a fiery ball of gas in the sky.

People on Earth would only think that the gods were angry with them, and they would hide or pray for forgiveness. It seemed unreal to be watching these awkward people, who were probably some of my ancestors or descendants.

The flying columns were able to move rapidly over the land and water at tremendous speeds while those aboard stood comfortably in an enclosed area. It was the standing order of the day for pairs of flying columns to travel together in alien or unoccupied areas outside the empire of Atlantis. The scenery, the mountains, and the colors were so inviting, even if this did happen thousands of years ago. The last part of the film summarized the places visited, the people observed, and what was accomplished on the mission.

Although I watched the film clip with keen interest, it was a mystery to me why some of the people on the ground in the lands visited did not wonder what these discernible objects were. Why wasn't anything ever written down or preserved in stone to note the intrusion or visitation of unidentified flying objects? Perhaps the society of the day was unconcerned with this happening.

After witnessing an actual account, I even fancied myself as being one of those persons flying over the European continent making visual observations and recording data. All of us, at one time in our lives, liked to think that it would be fun to be a hero. To be the idol of millions who are envious of success is often a true fantasy we all share. Imagine being aboard one of those flying columns moving discreetly over foreign lands, seeing strange people taking photographs, and eating exotic foods. It would have been thrilling to speak the language that may have been the predecessor of modern English and making history come alive through great works of art carved in stone throughout the Earth for future man.

Ideas pulsated through my brain as I witnessed the film documentary. I was somewhat spellbound by the experience.

Lambda Photon asked, "What do you think of us in light of this filmed sequence?"

"Dear, I find the experience totally overwhelming. Are there any other filmed documentaries similar to this one?"

She said, "I thought you were anxious to reach the surface of the city."

I quickly told her, "Under these circumstances, I'm in no hurry. After all, this series of events that has happened to me clearly points to the roots of our present civilization on Earth and in space colonies."

Once again I asked, "Are there other filmed documentaries?"

Immediately she replied, "Yes! Watch what happens when I press the second button twice."

This time the picture cleared, and another film sketch began. It showed the ascent of three flying columns leaving the city of Atlantis and flying westward. Somehow each of the flying machines could communicate with all the others.

Also, the flying column had a homing device that gave its exact position on each mission. If weapons were on board these crafts, they were not visible. I noticed that in each film clip all the people wore white tunic clothes and gold jewelry. This enabled us to speculate that the city was in a warm climate.

The particular flight on the film showed movement over the ocean and the sight of a great continent in full view. I wondered if North America was the destination as flights were always taken by day. There was also no attempt to reveal the source of propulsion.

The flight continued westward over great forests and rivers. The captain or centurion commander made the remark that no visible cities lay in view. Some mountain groups were visible as they continued toward the west. There were three sightings of Indian villages. The Atlanteans regarded these people as inferior even though they represented the only *Homo sapiens* visually observed and recorded through photography.

It was interesting to note that never once did the Atlanteans try to make verbal contact with any outsiders. Apparently, they were content just to study and keep a sharp lookout over the people on Earth.

No wonder the early people of the North American continent referred to religious tribal ceremonies as being visited by the "Great Spirit." The sight of these flying devices could easily have put fear into the heart of man.

Then the return flight to Atlantis across the ocean was shown. More attention was noted this time as the flying columns landed in Atlantis. The city was futuristic in architectural design. Buildings, dwellings, and superficial structures dominated the scope of the city. Large clear tubes with an enclosed monorail system provided transportation for the citizens.

Each building looked like the end of a giant rainbow with colors that marveled its beauty and richness. The film sequence then closed, and the picture faded. Then all I could see was one large stone with two buttons on it.

Lambda Photon could see the pleasure I derived from these scientific accounts and how I ached to learn more. Soon thereafter, I would achieve the ultimate mind-link of man's history. It was not the fact that I was being critical of Atlantean history. I felt there was more to decipher than superficial characters showing the ultimate power of Atlantean prowess and skill during their exploitation of the Americans and the European Continent.

Lambda Photon then asked me, "Are you ready to continue in your learning process or would you rather rush back to the surface of the city?"

"No, let's continue if you think we have enough time," I replied.

We continued walking through the corridors until we faced another stone wall. My inner thoughts automatically reacted to seeing Lambda Photon repeat the same ritual of opening the stone portal. I was beginning to expect these moves from her.

After a while, I thought the walls were moving as we approached the entrance to another part of the cave. I almost imagined myself an Atlantean in a subhuman form without body, possibly pure energy, yet in perfect harmony with the world around me. I almost reached the point where I could feel no pain or pleasure even through the eons of time and space.

Finally, the stone portal moved slowly to the left. Lambda Photon invited me to follow. As we proceeded through the enclosure, I again received a tingling sensation in my left ear that was bothersome. I thought, *Why am I different from anyone else? Why must I experience pain each time?* I wondered, *Is this some type of conditioning?*

After approximately ten seconds, the pain stopped. We walked through another corridor of the cave that appeared even more brightly illuminated. Lambda Photon led me to a much larger room that I assumed must be a museum filled with priceless treasures taken from the original city of Atlantis. The items were one-of-a-kind in the realm of present day civilization.

"Kit, you can touch the objects, but be careful as they are irreplaceable."

"I will handle everything with care, Lambda Photon."

Bubbling with curiosity of the unknown, I entered the room. Sitting on a short stone pillar was a vase with ornate pictures of people at a festival. It was multicolored and appeared to be a great work of art.

Another object on the wall was a painting of the city with people moving to and fro. I noticed the artist's name was Cantorian, which was similar to Cantor, the ruler of the New Empire. The oil painting was so lifelike that the people actually appeared to be moving. It was obvious the artist had captured the heart of realism in the portrait. I was envious of such a beautiful and fanciful place.

"Kit, the fine arts were an educational requirement of Atlantean children. They were taught to develop an appreciation for education and religion, thus eliminating crime and war as worrisome entities in a remarkably advanced society. Those who preferred science devoted themselves to developing and implementing all types of inventions. Others worked with defense or agricultural issues. Regardless of which path the students chose, they became prolific in their field of endeavor," commented Lambda Photon.

There was no doubt in my mind as I looked intensely at the portrait that I was rapidly becoming a part of Atlantean history.

I left the portrait and walked over to a silver and gold chalice. What special meaning was in its value as a museum treasure to be preserved forever? The beautiful chalice was heavy in my hand. I did not believe it was used for drinking purposes but to preserve history through antiquity. There was an enormous amount of symbolism on the beautiful chalice, unlike any signs I had ever seen or read about concerning ancient hieroglyphs.

I wondered if these symbols might be related to early forms of writing by the Sumerians who used cuneiform as a means of communicating messages. Lambda Photon observed my primitive attempts to analyze and investigate the origin and meanings of the unusual chalice. This time she made no attempt to interpret the meanings or show signs of helping me understand the symbolism.

Apparently, there was a secret hidden within the symbolism that I was not supposed to comprehend. I put the chalice in its proper place and walked over to a decorative box sitting in one part of the room on a gold leaf table with a white marble top. As I approached the table, Lambda Photon moved in front of me as if to block my path. I didn't wish for her to think I was upset because she abruptly blocked me; rather I moved around her toward the box.

Lambda Photon suddenly placed her hand on top of the box that resembled a small chest. At once, light energy passed upward from the box through her hand and toward the ceiling. It appeared to be pure energy moving toward the roof of the cave room. She seemed to rasp with pain as her face, mouth, and eyes showed agony. I started to move toward her to try and help, but she motioned me away. Suddenly, she cried out, "Kit, place both your hands on the table where the box is sitting."

As I did so, the energy being emitted by the box stopped. Lambda Photon quickly withdrew her hand and rubbed it vigorously.

"Thanks, Kit. I should have known better. The box has a defense mechanism connected to a sensor in the ceiling that activates when touched. I hope you realize now why I cautioned you earlier. I've been in this room before and never touched the box. I guess my curiosity got the better of me, and I made a bad choice."

"That's okay. We all make mistakes," I replied.

Still, I was curious concerning the nature of the seemingly harmless box which obviously was capable of producing vast energy.

Lambda Photon looked at me rather strangely and asked, "Kit, do you know the story of the Medusa?"

I told her as far as I knew, Medusa was a woman who had snakes that permeated from her head in all outward directions but remained forever attached to her head. Her eyes gave a piercing look at everything she observed. To look at her would cause any living creature to turn to stone. My educational background had always led me to believe the legend to be a Greek myth.

Surely, in my present existence, I never thought there would be a million-to-one chance of meeting this alien creature. Was I now expected to suddenly meet someone who was being mysteriously introduced by Lambda Photon? The legend of Medusa seemed to heighten my imagination, and my excitement grew as I wanted to learn more. *Am I destined to meet a counterpart of the actual woman?* I felt the answer probably lay in these catacombs of mysterious origins.

Suddenly, a thought-wave transmission meandered across the neuro-spinal fluid levels of my brain. The box must be the origin of Medusa's power, or simply Medusa herself. The power of Medusa had never been duplicated in history, as far as modern man knew. Not even the dreaded bombs of man or space weapons of alien origin could quite equal the transgressions of Medusa.

I laughed and thought it was too bad Cassandra of Troy was not here to predict the long and shortcomings of my destiny. I wondered if I might find myself a willing subject to bear the knowledge being imparted to me with the assistance of Lambda Photon as a cohort of the existing government. She used her highly developed extrasensory perception techniques to listen into the philosophical ideas that seemed trapped in my subconscious but neutral level of brainwave activity, mainly directed toward the period of certainty and realism.

I seemed a willing subject bent either on destruction or escape.

"Kit, do you realize you are overreacting to this situation? There are many things we have yet to learn. Eventually, our scientists will solve the problem."

I thought about what Lambda Photon had said for a moment. Apparently, this meant that the New Empire had never fully realized the potential power of the black box, or Medusa, as I labeled it.

I wondered what else I would find in this remarkable and intriguing place. Close to the entrance and exit there appeared to be a mechanical or electronic switch that had not been used for some time because of the dust surrounding the silicon casing. Was this another museum piece?

Lambda Photon watched me cautiously. I turned to face her, and as I did, her eyes met mine. "Kit, the silicon casings are indeed museum pieces. Be careful in handling these artifacts. They represent our early attempts to create light in a bulb mounted to a base, which was connected to a power source. Sometimes the light produced heat if left on too long. Over time the light bulb's silicon filament would get hot and begin to weaken and break, causing the light to extinguish."

"I understand perfectly, Lambda Photon."

Once again her eyes prevailed on me as one studying a baby's attempt to learn to walk. I wasn't totally baffled by the strange objects; however, I needed to appear devious in my thought-wave pattern to confuse Lambda Photon as to the nature or origin of these interesting objects. Inwardly, I felt that most of them were somewhat familiar and almost homely to the life I lived in Galaxy Fourteen.

Suddenly, a startling thought surfaced in my brain. Could these artifacts be a reunion with my past life from seven years of age onward? Could I be seeing things that were somehow created to make me believe I was coming home? Only then did I recall that I had thought earlier I felt I had known Lambda Photon previously, but not in the thirty-second century.

Was this truly a homecoming? I felt a smooth, warm hand touch mine as I looked around the room. My mind was collecting data from my life's history at rates only superseded by the speed of light. I wanted to turn and face this mystery person, but something seemed to prevent my movement.

The Revelation

It was not like the soft, silken hand of Lambda Photon but that of an aged, compassionate person. Was it Mother? Was it a relative unknown to me? Was it someone who touched my life only for a moment in time but seemed to help me decide my destiny?

The power surge to face that person increased within me. As I turned, the hand released mine very quickly and, in full view, I witnessed a spectacle for which I was unprepared. I thought I had seen everything in the room, but I was so wrong. There were no other people there except Lambda Photon and me. This seemed very weird. "Sweetheart, could you tell me where the person is who just touched me?"

She refused a reply and walked over to a flat-faced stone wall and placed her hand on an elevated platform. At once, a picture illuminated the screen. A computer-like voice monitored all pictures that emanated from the stone wall.

"Welcome, Lambda Photon. How can I help you?"

"My guest and I would like to ask some questions regarding the status of his life and experiences from early childhood until the present."

Excitement coursed throughout my body at the thought of learning more about my life. I wondered if this device could reveal to me the things I wanted to know, things I had not been able to secure from the records in Galaxy Fourteen.

How could a mechanism such as this tell the destiny of one's life unless it was supernatural?

"Kit, do not question the authenticity of the instrument. The computer is designed to complete a brain scan when you activate the platform. Study the information as it is provided for you. As pictures flash by, look for clues that might help you identify things that happened throughout your life. I only hope you can gather enough clues that you can begin to remember things that were suppressed so long ago."

Apprehension was evident as I had doubts and wondered if some device was devouring my thoughts stored from early childhood to the present. I was trying to be optimistic; however, it was difficult not to be skeptical at such a strange occurrence.

Lambda Photon then took my hands and clasped them in hers. She viewed me in a loving way and said, "Have faith and trust in me. You will learn much today."

These thoughts seemed to penetrate deep within my soul, and I felt as if this were one of those moments of truth and conviction. I released her hands, which seemed like chains broken from the bonds that held me tightly. I then walked over and slowly placed my hand on the elevated platform. At once, the rock glowed white, but not intensely enough to hurt my eyes.

"Lambda Photon, will the computer recognize me?"

"Yes, now be quiet and concentrate."

All at once a booming computer-like voice said, "Hello. Are you Kit Bartusch?"

"Yes, that's me."

"Now that your identity has been verified by the computer system, you are directed to watch the screen as your name and articles about your life will be displayed for your perusal," commanded the ominous voice.

I watched in amazement as my life story began with the statement of my birth in the year AD 2731. An account of my childhood from birth was then portrayed.

"Lambda Photon, look at the picture of that man and woman."

Across the screen the names John and Mary Bartusch were displayed beside the picture.

I am so thankful to learn I actually have real parents, but why can't I remember anything about them? I do resemble them. My hair, eyes, nose, and facial features are clearly identifiable.

Apparently, my dad had enjoyed watching old cowboy movies as numerous pictures on the screen showed his childhood hero was Kit Carson of the eighteenth-century. He liked the name Kit so much that I was named Kit because he felt I would be an adventurer or hero of space travel. How true to life I had become. Up to this point in time, I had more adventure and excitement in my life than all the space heroes in any book I had ever read. I was the first real time traveler to see and experience things not known in my own time.

From the pictures, it appeared that my mother was about 5 feet 5 inches tall with black hair and fair complexion. Dad also had black hair and stood about 5 feet 9 inches. I was fascinated with the way they looked. I touched my eyes, nose, chin, and hands, feeling the family resemblance.

Suddenly, there were so many questions I wanted to ask, even though this was a filmed sequence. I longed to touch and hold my parents while telling them of my many adventures from youth to the present. The picture of my parents holding me looked so loving. What I wanted so desperately to know was where they were and what had become of them since we were separated.

I felt like the great Lord Odysseus coming home to his wife, Penelope, as I gazed passionately at my real parents. Stunned as I was, I remained transfixed on the pictures. For some unexplained reason, I reached out toward Lambda Photon. She came toward me willingly as if she knew what I wanted her to do. I felt the need to show my love for Lambda Photon to my parents, although I knew it was impossible.

Hot flashes of blood surged within me as I felt this to be a genuine learning experience. From the knowledge I now had about my parents, I was better prepared for life. I knew I had a beginning from parents who loved me enough to protect me, although dangers plagued their existence in space.

From the available evidence, I learned that my parents had lived on a small planet in Galaxy Twelve. Dad was an astronomer, and my mother worked as a clinical pathologist in a nearby research institute. Dad was concerned about the movement of several comets that had penetrated Galaxy Twelve. They appeared to be moving toward our quadrant in space. One day when I was three years old, an alarm sounded throughout our living complex, warning of flying debris that would be moving across the morning sky within the next four hours.

Galaxy Twelve was not as technically advanced as the New Empire and had little or no defense against moving planetary bodies through space. Force fields were only experimental, and the thought of building one that could circumnavigate our galaxy was not feasible. Evacuation seemed the only escape.

There were just enough spaceships to carry the food, children, nurses, doctors, and a few select people. So, with their love for me, I was sent, and they remained on Galaxy Twelve, not realizing the true danger that lay before them. Our spaceships carried us to Galaxy Fourteen, where I remained under the care of Central Intelligence at a children's ward because of my quick ability to learn and achieve.

It was fascinating how all these events could have transpired in my life from childhood to the present, and now in this alien territory, I was being reunited with the past. I was proud to learn I had parents who loved me enough to give me up so that I might become happy and successful in life. Despite all that had transpired, finding out about my early childhood was a rewarding experience.

As the filmed sequence ended, I removed my hand and then glanced at Lambda Photon in a puzzled state. Tears filled my eyes and flowed onto my cheeks. I really wasn't nervous, though one couldn't help but wonder what echoed in my brain as I faced her.

The stillness that permeated the room seemed like an aura that hung over us in a permafrost state. It was unlike any experience I had ever known. Lambda Photon welcomed me back to reality.

Although I was a time traveler, I had found my new home. All the memories of the twenty-seventh century seemed unimportant and out of sequence with my present state of life. I placed my hand in hers and squeezed tightly.

Suddenly, I felt a searing passion and intimately embraced Lambda Photon for several minutes. No words were needed, as our thoughts were exchanged on high levels of extrasensory perception, and love seemed to conquer our innermost feelings.

These events had taken a mere space scientist of the distant twenty-seventh century and placed him five hundred years later into the true destiny of his life. I wondered why it was necessary to omit those five hundred years from all thought transmissions. Was I locked into suspended animation yet conscious of all knowledge being absorbed by mankind? Had I been recycled or refurbished to represent the highest order of human beings? These thoughts and many others seemed to illuminate my passion for success.

I released Lambda Photon's hand and looked once again around the strange cave. This had been a great day in the history of my life. The blueprint, or great plan of my life, had been released to me in a sort of fantasy like *Alice in Wonderland*.

Strangely, I wanted to sit down and recompose my thoughts. Close to the entrance sat a chair resembling a modified seat for relaxation. I was so ecstatic that I wanted to shout for joy. I jumped up, and taking both of Lambda Photon's hands, danced around the room gliding to and fro as if I had had a mental lapse or wonderful release of joy and happiness.

Two or three minutes later, I stopped and held her close. This time I experienced the type of love that only a man and woman could know forever.

She asked, "If I should ever call you, will you answer me?"

I replied, "Nothing could stop me."

Suddenly, all sorts of strange lights pulsated through the room, as if the walls had ears to hear and eyes to see. I felt strangely chilled, yet unafraid. A sort of lightning beam that originated from nowhere danced on the walls. I didn't have time to be puzzled or afraid, so I took Lambda Photon, and we cowered on our knees and dodged the dancing, lightning bolts.

I looked at Lambda Photon and said, "Have I offended you or the keepers of the cave museum?"

Before she could reply, the strange lights stopped and all seemed normal once again. We slowly got to our feet and regained our composure.

"Kit, the phenomena we just observed was that of a time traveler passing through his portal in the cave. I don't know how he locked into you, but he must have recognized you from the past."

I assume my question is satisfactory to the observer, and all is well.

I tried to prevent Lambda Photon from reading my mind, although it seemed futile. Was the time traveler my mother? Was she trying to tell me all was well and she was pleased with my selection of a mate for all eternity? I felt good thinking this was what truly must have happened.

Once again Lambda Photon read my thoughts instinctively and smiled. What did the future hold for me beyond the realm of my whereabouts? Time stood still for only an inkling of a second, and I had lived a lifetime in the cosmos of the unknown.

My journey through time had opened new vistas of life around me; however, everything at the moment seemed to eclipse my very being in my search for identity and truth.

Indeed the scales of justice seemed to balance in my favor for the moment. I delighted in the fact that I had succeeded where others had failed in their search for who they were and where they were going. Though time had seemed like an independent variable, it increased my appetite to inquire of my future through tranquil thought and exploration of the world in which I had become a part.

I was not a zealot or adventurer of romanticism, but a conscious air-breathing human seeking the lost identity of one so dear to me. I yearned to learn more yet only had to wait for the next event as the seconds seemed to fly by. Time had taken precedence in my life, and the truth was ominously present.

I was confused in many respects. It was as if I were only a discernible object to be toyed with—an object to be bounced back and forth between loyal partners.

Lambda Photon seemed to grasp the impenetrable thoughts from my conscious mind and shuffled them in a way that made them easy to comprehend. If she hadn't been there, I guess all this would have been meaningless to me in spite of finding out my true identity.

Lambda Photon's thoughts took control of the status of my thought-wave pattern. I knew inwardly that my thoughts needed adjustment or repair from the transcendental mental state I was in. I wanted to believe that I was in complete control of all my faculties, but everything I seemed to touch or look at took on new meaning and purpose in my life.

One thought seemed to beam through me as I looked about the cave museum in awe—*Escape this place of the past. Find out what is in store for me in the future.* Suddenly, I faced Lambda Photon and smiled. It had been many days since I had experienced an emotion such as this. The bitter pain of realizing my true identity seemed totally at ease in my present environment. Then I told Lambda Photon, "Let's continue our journey to the surface of the city."

Stone Portal

Taking her hand in mine, we left the cave museum through a large exit and proceeded through the stone corridor. We walked what seemed like perhaps fifty to seventy-five steps in silence. With an occasional glance at Lambda Photon, I had the need to satisfy my innate curiosity that she was indeed real and not a false image or mirage. The warmth that flowed from her hand to mine as we moved along seemed immeasurable. I felt truly safe with her, although there had been moments in my life when I wasn't totally sure and feared the unknown.

We came to some steps that seemed to rise upward. "Kit, do you feel the change in temperature? I think it's getting warmer."

I replied, "Yes!"

There was a light on the left side of the corridor adjacent to the steps, and Lambda Photon spoke directly to the light.

"Computer, this is Lambda Photon, daughter of Cantor. My companion is Kit Bartusch. We have just completed an extensive journey through the cave and need your help to travel toward the surface."

"Computer XTZ ready. I am at your command and will be more than glad to provide the necessary instructions. The first thing you need to do is make sure your companion does exactly as you say."

"Kit, did you hear what he said?"

"Yes, I'm listening."

Then she motioned for me to follow her and not to let go of her hand. It seemed like fifty steps before we came to a large, circular stone floor.

"Kit, we will now walk slowly over to the round stone floor. Once we get there, stand perfectly still, and do not say a word. Do you understand?"

"Yes."

"Lambda Photon, are we standing in the correct place?"

"Kit, don't say anything! You must remain silent!"

Immediately, I sensed we were moving upward toward the surface; however, I felt no movement. All at once, the pillar we were standing on stopped.

Lambda Photon grabbed my hand and said, "Kit, we must exit the flat pillar onto the rocky surface, and we have to do it very quickly."

We did so while continuing to hold hands. Just as we stepped off, the pillar descended into the depths of the planet only to be covered automatically by surface vegetation. It looked as if the landscape had appeared from nowhere. I was just glad to be back on the surface of the planet.

Then I began to wonder what we were doing on the surface of this planet. *Did we make a wrong turn underground and miss the underwater city of Atlantis? Am I to question Lambda Photon in her selection of the way to the city?* I did not think I could blame her for this so-called mistake.

I felt that somehow she would make all this up to me at a time that was meaningful to each of us. I also realized that I was in a strange place, and if I intended to survive, I would have to follow her advice to the letter.

We scanned the horizon in all directions. My thoughts seemed to give me away without gesticulating or speaking in a soft monotone. Lambda Photon had carefully monitored and dissected my conscious thought in a conventional way.

I wondered, *Where are we and how will we return to Cantor's estate?*

These thoughts seemed to enter Lambda Photon's mind, because she looked at me and placed both her hands on my shoulders. She said, "What if we can never return to my father's home? Will you then hate me for what I have done to us?"

I loved Lambda Photon, but the way she said this left a heavy burden in my heart. She had never lied to me as far as I could tell. What she spoke had to be the truth.

I felt the words take hold of my soul as the blood in my veins roared as if Father Time himself was in complete command of my destiny. I then told her, "We can make it if our love and faith remain bonded forever." Never before had we seemed so close to one another. Certainly, this had to be love that countless men seek in their search for the truth.

Placing my arms around her, I pledged my life to her. The tranquility of peaceful surroundings seemed to engulf us as we began a new journey toward the setting sun of this far and distant planet trillions of light-years from my own time. Life could never remain subtle and undivided again. I had found a new beginning and was eager for adventure into the twilight of tomorrow.

The setting sun seemed impenetrable in all its hue, drawing us nearer with many things still unexplained. I seemed to be drawn magnetically in the direction of the sun. I suppose that my expression resembled the little drummer boy looking at the toy castle in complete awe and majesty.

For some reason, I just knew this route was the immediate direction we would have to follow. *By her reaction, Lambda Photon feels the same as I do.* It was as if I had been predestined to go across the surface of this strange planet with no fear, yet with strength of mind.

Taking Lambda Photon's hand, I led her from our place of ascent and moved seemingly westward. The planet was dusty and visibility calculative. Large boulders seemed out of place in this particular segment of the planet. We walked past several boulders, only to find open land for a mile or two. I estimated the boulders to be of limestone with origin definitely not shaped by erosion. They looked as if they had been precisely cut to peculiar dimensions and thrown all over the surface to discourage would-be space travelers in this millennium of space travel.

As we walked, we were so entranced with the scenery that we spoke little as we observed the planet's surface in great detail. We came to a massive granite boulder shaped in the form of an equilateral triangle sitting perfectly upright. It appeared to be anchored without any support. We walked around it several times and placed our hands on the surface. As I looked at it, my mind conjured up all kinds of ideas. *Could this stone triangle unlock the future of our lives?*

I wasn't afraid; however, things that I had forgotten as a child could be sensed. Lambda Photon rapidly scanned my thoughts as if on the frequency of a binary computer of the series four alpha. She could transcribe the thoughts as fast as I thought them, singly, then in multiples. I told her, almost in a joking way, that in all my curiosity, I had forgotten my bodily need for hunger. Carefully, she took out two space food capsules for us to consume, thus eliminating our hunger pains.

"Lambda Photon, are we far enough away from your civilization that we cannot be detected?"

"Yes, Kit. The rocky surface we are in places us under radar."

"Lambda Photon, now is the time for us to discuss our options."

"Do you rejoin your family and continue as before or do you want to remain with me? I want you to think seriously about the decision you are making. I know it is the toughest one you will ever have to make. It's almost impossible to give up your family, as they love and care for you. As the firstborn, you could easily succeed them as queen in the event of their deaths."

"Looking at this dilemma another way, if you decide to stay with me and get caught trying to leave, then your demise is certain. If we are lucky and do not get caught, we can possibly travel far enough to remove ourselves from their civilization and start a new life together."

"Kit, I've thought about the different options and have made my decision. I can't bear going through life without you. My love for you is endless."

"Lambda Photon, I love you too. If you're sure of your decision, then let's continue our journey through this area. Hopefully, there will be ample time for us to become even closer in the days ahead. Should we be discovered, you can always say you were simply showing me the surrounding area."

We sat down at the edge of the massive stone triangle. For some unexplainable reason, I reached my hand into my pants pocket and felt keys. The only time that I remembered having keys was as a youth. I slowly removed them and held them away from my face. The tinkling sound of keys rattling revived old memories of life back at the space academy in Galaxy Fourteen. Thought processes entered my mind, just as if an alarm had sounded on the space portal air locks. *Could this stone triangle be the key to the next dimension or lead us in the direction of a parallel universe that seems only superficial in the minds of scientists and controversial astronomers?*

Lambda Photon's curiosity of the keys seemed as intense as mine. We looked at the coded numbers on each of the keys. I tried to relate each one to a segment of my life. Once again, she read my mind with exact precision.

Another idea entered my mind. Could this be a time portal? I was intrigued by this transient thought of great intensity and seemed to be drawn toward the stone triangle. I turned and scanned the great face of the stone. To my right, about two meters away, appeared a door with a key hole. I felt as if I were losing my mind because Lambda Photon and I both looked around the massive structure and never once observed the stone door. However, there it was, and I knew it had something to do with my life, perhaps both our lives.

Once again, a feeling overcame me to look at the keys. Apparently, the keeper of the portal was trying to make it known to me that one of the keys could unlock the door. I was currently a time traveler and seemed content in my present situation. But, if I opened the stone door, would we be swallowed up by unknown realms of the future, or would we be swept away into the parallel universe, becoming only a fragment of time lost forever in a microcosm of self-identity and exploration?

All these thoughts simply would not let my mind rest. Was I on the highest level of thinking? Would I change from keeping the same identity in my so-called next life?

The door and key were obviously designed on levels that a human being could use. I faced Lambda Photon and posed another question, "Do you think we should unlock the stone portal and enter?"

She looked at me in a rather puzzled way and then replied, "What if we open the door and find it is only a closet filled with documents and armaments?"

"Lambda Photon, the way I see it, we really don't have much choice. Do you agree that we should go forward with our plan?"

"Yes, Kit. I will do as you say."

In an optimistic state, I began an interrogation of the situation. I carefully thought of the pros and cons of entering or opening the door. I wondered, *What will we find once the door opens? If we decide not to open the door, will it offend the keeper of the stone portal?*

I looked across the horizon and observed that the sun had set, and night was approaching. The surface temperature was somewhere between 70-80 degrees

Fahrenheit. The stone triangle seemed to glow in the dark as if it required my total attention.

"Lambda Photon, I need you to move two meters away from the stone."

Doing so, I then surprised her by speaking directly to the massive stone triangle.

"Why are you here?" Nothing happened. Again I spoke, "We are seeking the truth of the stone portal. Are we asking too much of one so great who has stood the test of time?"

Suddenly, a sound was emitted by the portal. "You have been given the keys to life eternal. Do not attempt to foretell your destiny. It was decided for you eons of centuries ago. Rise up and take the black key to the stone door, and do not be afraid to enter. By conventional standards, you have succeeded where others have failed."

A feeling of rapture surrounded us. It was as if heaven itself had lifted a great burden from our lives. Our decision was made. "Lambda Photon, are you ready?"

"Yes, Kit. Let's go."

Taking the black key in my hand, we walked up to the door, inserted it, and then turned the key to the right; the door screeched open very slowly.

When it was at a 90-degree angle, we began our entrance into the stone portal that was dimly lit and filled with a catacomb of tunnels. We had moved about ten to twelve feet when the door automatically shut behind us. The tunnel we entered had phosphorescent rock that provided ample light for us to see. We continued walking until we came to a room shaped in the form of a Y. Our path led us to the intersection of two other tunnels. I wondered, *Are our thoughts being monitored?*

"Stop where you are, Lambda Photon! We must decide which way to proceed. On what basis do you think our decision needs to be made?"

"I really don't know, Kit, but let's take it slowly."

I began to evaluate possible solutions to our situation. Once again, I spoke inside the labyrinth stone walls, "We seek the truth and meaning of life in peaceful co-existence with God and man, man and woman. We have not come to bear false witness or to relate poor judgment on mankind. We seek our destiny as deemed by our forefathers and given by God."

When I had finished a brief moratorium of the truth, stillness permeated the room unlike any other I had observed. I expected us to be struck by lightning or emphatically swallowed by the immense stone walls that appeared to move at the sound of human voice.

A commanding and resolute voice began an oratory that made us a witness to our faith and love for one another. The voice began: "You seek the truth of millions of men all over the universe. You have given and received wise counsel in your many endeavors as a time traveler. You have been given the love of one very dear and sincere. You have weighed many decisions and found many truths. The door to your life lies in your path. Either tunnel will take you directly to your destiny. Be not afraid, Kit Bartusch, for the questions and answers of life are as simple as the setting sun of Galaxy Fourteen. Do not hesitate or delay your journey.

Begin your new life with Lambda Photon. I will prepare the way, the truth, and the life for you. You have only to ask, and it will be given to you."

Taking Lambda Photon's hand in mine, we then began our journey through the twilight of the future with peace, harmony, and contentment pervading our lives. I had received very deep and wise counsel in an unseen voice that offered what I had wanted all my life, so it seemed.

The information had been revealed in the lives of two mere space travelers. What lay at the end of the tunnel that could possibly be so revealing and fortuitous?

The Forest

We walked onward until another door appeared. As Lambda Photon looked at me, her eyes revealed the same thoughts I had. I grabbed hold of the door handle, and with a slight turn to the right, the door then moved 90 degrees to the left. Sheer energy was being beamed down straight in front of us. It resembled the same yellow, dense light that we experienced as we began our descent into the mysterious cave. Lambda Photon took the initiative this time and tugged at me to move onward.

We stepped through the door and were immediately covered by the yellow light. The color was so intense that we both resembled two gold nuggets. Our skin looked as if it had been baked on. I surmised that we stood there for a few seconds, perhaps in awe of each other's appearance. We then walked out of the yellow light onto a clear and sunny planet.

All at once, the yellow color fragmented on contact with the atmosphere of the planet. I imagined this to be Mt. Olympus or perhaps even heaven. I wondered if my imagination was playing tricks on me. I toyed with the idea of having angel wings and a harp, but that was sheer fantasy. I asked, "Lambda Photon, are you okay?"

She said, "Yes, what about you?"

"I'm fine," I replied.

As for my arms and face, physically, I seemed to be okay. I noticed our bodies looked blurred, except for Lambda Photon's face. I asked, "Do you have the same problem?"

"Kit, you must be having another radiation attack from the yellow light."

I said, "Oh, no! Not again." Then I passed out.

Upon awakening a short while later, I detected no blindness; my eyes were normal, except for a slight twitch in the left one. Maybe it was because I felt nervous from the experience.

Lambda Photon had told me earlier that I had been conditioned to semi-evolved solar systems as part of my training for the New Empire. Maybe I was just lucky there wasn't anything else wrong with me other than a slight twitch of the eye.

For approximately ten minutes, I remained in a reclining position and then began to sit up slowly. Lambda Photon touched my forehead with hands soft as silk. Her hair was golden like grains of wheat, and she was smiling. I smiled back, and she asked, "Are you ready to continue our journey?"

"If you are," I replied.

I stood up and scanned the horizon where a sparsely populated forest lay directly ahead. To our right was also a large lake. On our left was forestland as far as the eye could see with birds flying overhead. The triangular stone portal was nowhere in sight.

"Lambda Photon, where is the stone portal?" *Could it just vanish?*

"Kit, you may not remember, but you passed out immediately after returning to the surface of the planet. You will be back to normal in a few minutes. As for the stone portal, we left it behind when we entered the cave."

I knew I had to make a decision. Should we travel across open land or go through the forest? Inwardly, I yearned to go through the forest. My secret desires were flooded with curiosity as Lambda Photon used her perceptive powers with finesse.

"Kit, I've never been in a forest. If we decide to go that direction, what am I to expect? Will it be scary? Should I be afraid of anything?"

"Well, for one thing, it will not be a fun experience. Forests have trees with leaves and animals of all types, including the carnivorous variety. Insects are everywhere. Some of the animals are nocturnal, and others are awake by day. Since you've never actually walked through a forest, you would have to remain close to me, as predators would be lurking around during both day and night hours. We would try to avoid dangers like snakes, lizards, foxes, wolves, and lions. However, there is always a possibility we might encounter dangerous obstacles."

"Lambda Photon, do you understand the dangers involved with these creatures as they hunt their prey for food? I know all this may sound crude to you, but you have to realize one creature eats another, and it becomes a never-ending cycle in the forest. Are you sure you still want to travel through the forest?"

"I like adventure, and I believe we are both prepared to face whatever adversities we might encounter."

"Okay then. The forest is our destination."

Once again, I had a strange urge to check my

pockets for a clue to our next adventure. This time I found five fire sticks, two V-shaped pins used to detect radiation, a pocketknife, a key, and a whistle. I thought these items almost childish but perhaps somewhat practical in going through a forest. In my shirt pocket I found a written message that said, "Miracles do happen sometimes to those who keep the faith."

I wondered if Lambda Photon's thoughts had been transcribed to paper and placed in my pocket when I was unconscious. I read the message again and looked up at her. She was beaming with enchantment and happiness. Confidently, she said, "If we are to meet our destiny today, let's get started immediately."

She was beginning to sound and think like me. Maybe my earthly emotions were beginning to rub off on her. She seemed to pride herself on being a forceful and dynamic individual, capable of leadership and decision.

We began our walk toward the wooded forest. The sounds we heard were like those of an earthly forest in Galaxy Fourteen. We walked through the brush, knocking off the briers and leaves that seemed to stick to our clothing. I observed wild game everywhere. There were squirrels running over the branches of the trees at a playful gait. Once I even saw a deer and pointed it out to Lambda Photon, who showed no fear of any of the creatures thus far. I knew the first time human beings see a wild animal they are usually frightened, but Lambda Photon exhibited little or no emotion.

A small clearing appeared next to a lake, and I decided this would be a good place to rest and observe the countryside. After gathering some sticks and brush, a small fire was started. The temperature wasn't cold, but since we were in a strange place, I didn't know what to expect from the weather or animals we might encounter.

"Lambda Photon, just to be on the safe side, you need to arm your weapon, should we have the misfortune of being attacked by wild animals."

"Kit, my weapon is always armed and ready to fire."

"Sweetheart, I'm alerting you because I love you so much and don't want either of us to get hurt or killed. Sometimes our mere presence in the forest is enough to keep the animals away."

"Kit, what's that howling sound?"

"Dear, it could be a wolf or coyote. They are carnivorous and nocturnal hunters."

"Kit, there it is again. It seems to be getting closer to us."

"Lambda Photon, draw your weapon immediately, but do not fire it randomly."

"Kit, what are those furry-looking animals just ahead of us? They don't appear to be dangerous, but they keep looking at us with those piercing eyes."

"Sweetheart, those animals are wolves. Don't fire at them unless it appears they will attack us. Are you afraid?"

"Kit, all the other animals have appeared harmless. Look, those wolves are running toward us, moving so fast. What should I do?"

"Fire your weapon now!"

Zap, zap, zap went the weapon.

"Kit, I've destroyed all the creatures. Do you think other wolves will attack us?"

"Lambda Photon, I pray they will stay away. However, to be on the safe side I will burn the wolves

138 | Joe Fitzpatrick

and the putrid smell should keep other creatures away from us for a while. We'll cover all evidence with leaves and dirt before we leave."

"Kit, I'm still frightened. Do you think that other creatures will return and attack us?"

"Sweetheart, I will build two more campfires forming an equilateral triangle. We will position ourselves in the middle between the campfires for protection."

"Oh, Kit, you have such good survival instincts."

"Lambda Photon, would you watch for unwanted creatures while I gather some wood to quickly get the campfires burning?"

"Sure, Kit, and I'll also keep my weapon ready just in case other predators are sighted."

We sat down on the forest floor between the small campfires and began to reminisce about our previous adventures. I asked, "Lambda Photon, are you having second thoughts about me and the fact that you've left your home and family?"

"I have pledged my life to you, and where you go, I will follow."

What a wonderful thing to say, even if we were millions of parsecs from the former life in Atlantis. The sun had reached the zenith, and the lake reflected the light toward us. I wondered what lay ahead.

"Lambda Photon, this has been an interesting day. I pray to God often and ask him to safeguard our steps through every encounter we face. We've been more than lucky thus far. I really believe that God has guided us safely to this place, which for all purposes, might be the garden of Eden."

"Why do you say that, Kit?"

"From the time I can remember as a youth, the garden of Eden was a place of God. He decided to create a man and eventually created a woman so they could share and each would have a companion. Their names were Adam and Eve. It was the perfect place to live—free of pain, aging, and sin. It was a sacred place where one could have fellowship with God."

"Kit, what happened to it?"

"God told Adam and Eve the one thing they could not do was eat the fruit of the tree of knowledge of good and evil. Eve was tempted by a snake in the tree, and she ate the fruit, thus forever making the human race mortal instead of immortal."

"Why didn't she listen to God's warning, Kit?"

"The snake told Eve that when she tasted the fruit, she would become an equal with God. Greed always causes contempt with God, sweetheart. Over time God forgave them, but they and their descendants remain mortal until the time of death. At that time, I believe our souls will go to heaven and reunite with our loved ones in the presence of God. I know this is a lot for you to comprehend right now. Just think about all I've told you, and we will both pray that God will reveal the destiny of our life together."

My thoughts began to wander as we sat motionless within the confines of the small campfires. How would we secure food for our bodily needs? In a few days we would eventually run out of space food capsules, and therefore the need to locate food to sustain us was imminent.

Communication with other aliens on this planet was nonexistent for the time being. Lambda Photon's needs would become evident if she were to survive in a strange environment. I began to think negatively. The mere thought of survival taunted my inner self despite the warm and sensitive message given us by the triangular stone portal.

Our situation needed strong leadership, and I knew that my inner thoughts would be subject to recapitulation if I allowed myself to think along these lines of mediocrity. Getting up from a sitting position and walking over to the edge of the clearing by the lake, I looked from one end to the other, almost half-expecting to see someone I knew. With intense feelings, I tried to imagine positive meetings with friends and relatives that reflected good times shared together.

Lambda Photon also got up and walked over to me. "Kit, are you looking for something special?"

"Not anything really, sweetheart."

We looked out over the water and noticed the ripples reflecting the strength and magnitude of the brightest star in the sky. However, when we looked at the ripples for an extended time, they seemed to play tricks on our eyes.

"Lambda Photon, is this truly the first time you have ever seen nature in its natural form?"

"Yes," she replied.

There was something magnetic yet unclear about the forest. I felt at home, but there seemed to be a cloud in my memory of what this place meant in the transition of my life from youth to adulthood.

"Lambda Photon, have you ever gone someplace for the first time and felt as if you knew everything about it?"

"No, Kit, I can't say that I have, although I guess it might be possible."

I just have a weird feeling, almost like I have been here in the past. It gives me cold chills. *Is it possible for me to have a precognition of these phenomena?* I couldn't really believe this setting and events that we experienced were left entirely to chance.

All at once, I felt a strange buzzing in the temple area on both sides of my head. It had been days since I had experienced the unusual occurrence. The pain was excruciating, and I cried out, "Why me, Lord? Why me?"

The buzzing lasted about ten seconds and then ceased. I sank to a sitting position with my hands on my head, reeling from the pain.

Lambda Photon took both her hands and placed them on the temples of my head. I felt a very cold sensation from her fingertips, much like a cool compress being applied for a headache. Seemingly, the coolness permeated my skull to the cerebrum, and I immediately relaxed.

"Kit, sit quietly for a moment and let me get you a pill I have in my bag. Here, swallow this. It will help to relieve the pain."

I closed my eyes and saw the color red. Maybe the capsule increased my blood flow, and what I was experiencing was true to nature. I trusted Lambda Photon to help me. We remained there a short time as the campfires died down, and we were able to resume our journey through the forest. Before leaving we erased all evidence of our having been there.

After completing the task, we continued walking until the brush seemed to become exceedingly dense. I noticed the trees got thicker in diameter at their base and there was a presence of pinecone bristles.

The sun was sinking low on the horizon, which meant that night was rapidly approaching. Safety was my primary concern, and the fear of the unknown creeping up on us also didn't exactly set my mind at ease.

I found a tree that was heavily branched and decided we would be safer if we climbed higher above the ground without any campfire to draw unpleasant or unwanted creatures toward us. Besides, the branches were very leafy, and their colors would camouflage us for the night.

Lambda Photon was reluctant to do as I asked and appeared to be developing new fears.

"Kit, I've never climbed a tree. I'm afraid once I get up there, I'll fall during the night."

"Sweetheart, you have to trust me."

She finally agreed, and we found our way to a large branch, wide enough and strong enough to hold our weight.

"Lambda Photon, we've climbed sufficiently high enough to keep lions and other predators away from us. Try to relax. I'm right beside you and will not let you fall."

Using my knife, I broke some small branches away and formed a makeshift pillow. Also, I took a large vine and tied it around us and to the tree limb so we would not fall during the night.

"Kit, aren't you worried about our situation?"

"No, darling. We're safe for now. I'm holding you securely in my arms. Close your eyes and relax. You have nothing to fear tonight."

Please God, I pray that you will keep us safe from all harm.

As we lay there, the twilight of night seemed to engulf our souls, and we sank into a stupor of sleep.

Once during the night I awakened; however, I was able to resume my sleep very peacefully. The morning sun thrust its shadow upon us, waking us on our lofty perch. I gently untied the vine, and we sat up slowly, stretching our arms and enjoying the refreshed feeling from a good night's rest.

The forest beneath us looked exactly the same as the previous day. All the sounds remained consistent with the occasional screech from a bird high in the sky seeking out a distant prey for dinner. The morning dew on the leaves and on our lips revealed a succulent taste that was inconsistent with all the other forests I had visited.

Maybe it was this transfiguration of knowledge that prepared the way for our unmapped journey. Today was a new beginning, and we were eager to continue on our journey as we climbed out of the tree and made our way through the forest. Life seemed more exciting for a change. Would this new beginning become reality?

Cave under the Waterfall

We worked our way through the maze of trees and were constantly besieged by small, intertwined branches that plagued us as we moved through the forest. I tried not to show any emotion or discomfort as the branches continued to hit our faces. We walked about a mile and stopped beside one of the largest tree trunks we had seen thus far. Sitting for a moment, we wiped the sweat from our brows as the walk had definitely caused us to use up much of our energy.

Suddenly, I heard something. *What can it be?* I had to warn Lambda Photon. We might be in danger. "Lambda Photon, be very quiet, do not speak and listen. I just heard an unfamiliar noise."

The sounds of the forest seemed to overshadow the presence of both of us in our metallic suits.

"Do you hear that rumbling sound, Lambda Photon?"

She replied, "Yes! What is it?"

"I don't know, possibly a waterfall."

We got up and moved steadily through the tangled brush toward the magical sound. Approximately thirty minutes later, we reached a cannonade of water boiling downward into foam, which took on the illusion of a water fountain of majestic proportions. We stood in awe of its omnipotent presence.

I was somewhat spellbound by the sight. It was like reading about a place in my world and then going there for the first time and seeing it. At once, I observed a torn fragment of Lambda Photon's uniform where a bleeding flesh wound was exposed. I didn't know whether she was aware of it, so I reached into my pocket, got a cloth, and walked over to the edge of the foam that turned into clear, sparkling water and wet half of it.

After squeezing out the water, I then went over to Lambda Photon, whose eyes seemed bent on the majestic heights of the waterfall.

I didn't want to scare her so I said, "Sweetheart, you need to sit down for a few minutes."

"What's wrong, Kit?"

"Your uniform is torn, and you're bleeding."

"What do you mean, I'm bleeding?"

I realized that she had never seen a flesh wound with bleeding in her lifetime, so I explained to her that the wound had to be cleaned and wrapped so it would not be exposed to the elements. She watched in awe, showing no signs of discomfort as I dressed the wound.

Looking at the running water made each of us thirsty. We walked over to the water, bent down, cupped the water with our hands, and drank our fill. We were very thirsty but not overwrought by our journey through the forest.

My feet were hot in the boots I wore, so I removed them and placed my feet in the soothing, cool water. "The water feels wonderful. Take off your boots, sweetheart, and let your feet soak in the refreshing water."

She gave me a funny look but slowly removed them and carefully placed her feet in the whirling waters. I half expected her to withdraw her feet, but they remained as mine did. I speculated this was a first-time experience for her.

Maybe she was reading my mind as she smiled warmly and winked at me. We sat there, perched on a rock, with our feet in the water for about five minutes when I thought I heard something move directly overhead. It looked like a projectile or missile move across the sky, spanning one horizon to the other, thus placing us in the middle.

"What a thunderous noise I heard just above us! Hurry and put on your boots, and we'll move quietly to the edge of the forest so we cannot be seen."

"I'm scared, Kit. That sound is so loud."

"Lambda Photon, is this the first time you've ever heard a loud noise?"

"Yes, Kit. Do you know what the noise is?"

"No, I don't know, but we need to move someplace where we will not be seen. Come quickly."

I didn't know what to expect and had no desire to become an unwilling participant in war games for which Lambda Photon and I were obviously unsuited.

At the edge of the forest, I noticed a small cave entrance lying close to the waterfall. There was a partially covered area with water in front of the cave.

"Look straight ahead of us, Lambda Photon. There's an opening near the waterfall. We can hide in there in case of attack by unknown aliens. Hurry, walk quickly!" As I followed her toward the cave, I looked behind me constantly. This occurrence was an unknown that frightened me.

"Stay close beside me, darling. I couldn't stand it if we were to become separated against our will."

"Neither could I, Kit."

Carefully, we climbed into the small cave. I was afraid to build a fire, which might attract attention. The cave was dry, and we lay down on the rocky floor to rest. I lay close to the entrance so I could watch any movement near the waterfall. The appearance of night seemed to fall hours before it was due. Thus far, we had not heard any more noise. Exhaustion overcame us, and we both fell into a deep sleep.

Our rest seemed short in comparison to our previous night aloft in the trees. I awakened only to glance out at what appeared to be nighttime as the flickering starlight gave off a magical aura.

How awkward and out of place I felt as I lay there. I turned and looked at Lambda Photon. She was lying on her side adjacent to me. Even at night, her beautiful blonde hair seemed radiant and glowing. I realized that never before had I taken time to study and observe her in this fashion.

The tear in her body suit could be seen easily. Although occasional dirt and dust adorned her suit from her shoulders to her boots, she was very beautiful and alluring. It seemed as though I had reserved these thoughts for just such a time. I scanned her body for any visual side effects that our journey or the atmosphere might have inflicted. Her olive skin seemed unscathed.

I suppose that all the brain wave activity I directed toward her awakened her kinesthetic cues to the real world. She stirred in her sleep, and I didn't know if this was normal or abnormal in her repose, but it caught my full attention.

Slowly, she opened her eyes and called my name, "Kit! Kit! Where are you?"

Taking my hands and placing them on her shoulders, I said, "I'm right here beside you. You must have been dreaming. You're okay. Now go back to sleep."

I found myself totally awake and unable to reconsider sleep. My thoughts seemed to wander elsewhere as once again I looked out into the dark of night.

I listened to the night sounds for about fifteen minutes when suddenly I noticed raindrops falling in cut-time rhythm, each drop pouncing on the forest floor and beginning its descent into the water-laden pool of the waterfall. The rain began to pour hard, then harder, as it pelted the outlying forest.

It had been months since I had last observed rain. I was thankful the rain seemed to obscure any starlight, so I decided it was safe to use the fire stick and build a small fire. The warmth erased the damp environment created by the rain and also illuminated the cave. I felt a strange warmness created by the light as it projected imaginary images on the walls of the cave.

I looked up at the ceiling, only to observe another level that probably led to deeper depths within the cave. I thought, *Can I find a way to ascend to the higher level and explore the area?*

Like an adventurer eager for action, I began to search for ways to reach the next level. I noticed a series of protruding rocks that could be manipulated while climbing to the higher level.

My shuffling around inside the cave awakened Lambda Photon. She stirred in her sleep, raised her head, and asked, "Kit, what are you doing?"

"Watch me, dear." Then, I began to climb the rocks toward the next level.

She cried, "Be careful, Kit!"

"Don't worry, I'll be all right."

Reaching with both hands and one step at a time, I managed to advance to the next rock. Pulling my weight upward on a wall that was almost vertical was a new experience. There were times when I thought the skin would tear from my fingers. The ledge of the upper level was still a foot above me. I thought, *I must hold on. I can make it!*

With my right hand, I reached for the upper level. I found an exposed rock that seemed firmly embedded in the wall and swung my body toward another rock on which to support my feet. During the first attempt, my feet missed the exposed rock. To prevent falling, I grabbed hold of the ledge with my left hand to help sustain my weight. I kicked with my foot until I felt a slight indentation in the rock and placed my foot in it. Then I pulled myself upward and onto the higher level.

I looked into the blackness and only saw another segment leading deeper into the cave. My curiosity for additional exploration was strengthened.

"Lambda Photon, I need your help. Would you throw the lighted fire stick up to my level so I can explore the surrounding area?"

"Yes, but are you sure of what you're doing?"

"Yes, I'm sure." I knew I had to also get her up to this level, but I was afraid for her to climb the wall of rock. *I think I've figured out a way to get her up to me.*

My clothing and the few essentials I had on me would be the only way I could bring her upward. "Lambda Photon, for us to continue our exploration of the cave, I must devise a way to get you up to the level where I am now. I don't think you will be able to climb the wall as I did. The only item long enough to reach you is my pants leg. I will need for you to try and reach the leg of the pants so I can pull you upward. Do you understand?"

"Yes, Kit. I will try."

She took me seriously and followed my orders. Holding onto my belt, I lowered the pants to her. She jumped toward them, only to miss on her first attempt. Once again, I slung the pants downward. This time she used the wall of rock as a springboard to reach the pants. "Great! Hang on tightly, and I'll slowly pull you upward."

It took several minutes, but I finally was able to bring her up to the next level.

She smiled and even laughed at me in my half-naked condition. Quickly, I put my pants on and latched my space belt. I took the fire stick in my hand, and we began to walk through the cave. From all indications, the cave had been hollowed out by water, possibly even a river.

Obviously, it had been centuries since anyone had walked this path through the cave. I almost shuddered at the thought of encountering space monsters or creatures whose only concern lay in the food chain. We certainly couldn't run from them. A fifteen-foot drop-off would kill or injure us. We walked slowly through the cave until we came to a metal door with a keyhole. Instinctively, I reached into my pocket and felt the key I had used to open the door in the stone portal. I wondered if the key would also open this door.

What can I do? I must make a rational decision on whether to use the key in my pocket. I thought for a moment. I even looked at Lambda Photon, and as our eyes met, her thoughts seemed transfixed on mine. There appeared to be some hesitancy, as a certain amount of doubt and curiosity lay manifold in her expression of concern.

I looked at the key that resembled a pass key used to open a castle door, except on a smaller scale. Again I observed the unusual door that seemed cross-laced in iron.

Thoughts began to race through my mind with the quickness of lightning. I knew that I had to try the key in the door, just to satisfy myself. Carefully, I placed the hub of the key into the socket and turned clockwise. In doing so, the great metal door slowly opened. We were almost spellbound as we gazed into the room and noticed an intense golden hue. The walls of the cave were producing their own energy of phosphorescent light.

As we entered the room and crossed into a dimly lit adjoining room, the cave appeared to end. In this particular room was a central light with what appeared to be space relaxers or crew chairs aboard a spaceship for interplanetary travel. The black padding on the crew chairs looked to be very comfortable.

Between the two chairs lay a panel with an array of circuits and buttons. We approached the two space relaxers with caution. It appeared to us that the panel could be monitored for space travel, perhaps even time travel.

A tingling sensation enveloped my spine as I observed the circuits and panel buttons. Was this my ticket home to Galaxy Fourteen? Did I even want to return home? Could Lambda Photon accept the unusual circumstances? How would I explain my disappearance from the *Fanfare* and sudden reappearance back home millions of light-years away from my present existence in space?

Maybe all these ideas were mere pipe dreams. Perhaps this panel only monitored nerve stimuli in response to external temperatures or sensations of pleasure or pain.

"I don't want us to get separated, Lambda Photon. Whatever is causing me to pass out is…" *Oh no! Not again! Please, this can't be happening to me now!* My subconscious seemed to grasp my very being and cast clouds of gloom over me.

I could hear Lambda Photon speaking to me in a compassionate voice. "Forget the past! We have each other. That's all that matters. Don't worry. We'll get through this together. I have great faith in you."

These were reassuring words, and the gloom of my past thoughts seemed to dissipate like dry leaves before the wind. A sense of well-being dominated me as I regained consciousness and approached the mysterious panel with a sense of rationale.

I knew at that moment that God had answered my prayers. I loved her with all my heart. She had become the love of my life, so I looked into her glowing eyes and said, "I will never leave you."

Walking over and standing beside her, I got down on my knee and looked up at her and said, "Lambda Photon, there is no way I can go through the remainder of my life without you. Will you pledge your life to me for as long as we both shall live?"

With tears in her eyes, she took my hands and said, "I'm yours forever." I wondered, *Does she know what her acceptance really means for both of us?*

"Lambda Photon, you do realize I'm asking you to marry me?"

"Yes, Kit. There's nothing that can separate us now. My heart is yours to hold as long as we both shall live."

At this point, I took my Space Academy ring off my finger and placed it on hers signifying our engagement. She seemed confused and asked, "Why did you put your ring on my finger?"

"Darling, I don't have an engagement ring to give you, so I placed my service ring on your finger, signifying that we are to be married."

For a moment I thought I had done something terribly wrong. I even thought she might not accept my ring. "Lambda Photon, can you tell me what I did wrong?"

"Oh, Kit, it is not that you have done anything wrong. We just celebrate differently on our planet.

People get married and wear matching insignia on their clothing signifying they are married."

"You know I can accept those symbols of our love. I didn't realize what protocol to follow. One major concern I do have is whether our marriage will be performed under the auspices of God, the father, or many gods, honoring the New Empire?"

"Kit, we will develop our vows in a way that both of us agree to everything." To seal our agreement, we kissed and held each other for a long time.

Lost in Time

It wasn't the fact that failure to succeed was present, but the thought of returning home or traveling in time once again seemed to remove the aura that enshrouded my very being as I observed the control buttons on the complex panel. My heart pounded rapidly as I prepared to depress a red button on the left side of the panel. I pressed downward and the panel lit up.

The speaker came on and a computer voice activated. "Welcome to the present locale. Press the nearest green button, and observe the light image beamed from the panel onto the wall of the cave."

Instantly, the picture reflected the keeper of the cave. He was a man dressed like a futuristic space explorer. He was light-skinned, and his body was covered with protective clothing from the hazards of space or time travel.

Once again the computer voice sounded, "You have little to fear from the keeper. Your speech patterns are being monitored, and the keeper will reply to you as needed."

At that moment, the keeper said, "What is the nature of your business?

"We are lost in time," replied Lambda Photon.

She proceeded to tell of our many adventures since rising to the surface of her home planet. The keeper seemed highly impressed with the finite details of our experience as she attempted to explain our sequential journey.

I could tell that Lambda Photon was getting totally exasperated with the keeper, so I spoke and reassured him that what she had related to him of our journey was the truth.

Once again he asked, "How did the two of you arrive at this destination?"

Very calmly, I replied, "It was purely by chance."

He seemed somewhat satisfied with my answer. He then asked, "How may I help both of you?"

Lambda Photon and I looked at each other and then faced the keeper without uttering a word. He replied, "So, that's what you want! You want to seek your destiny in life!"

"Yes," we replied. "That is correct, but how did you know?" He just smiled and said, "I know all things in the realm of time and space."

We then asked him, "Why are you locked up here if you know everything?"

He said, "In good time all will be explained to you. Your time of learning is but an inkling of space dust cast before the transient suns of distant star systems."

"Keeper, does this mean we are just beginning to understand the cosmos by way of our journey through time?"

"The only thing I can tell you is not to look back to the past, but look forward and seek the truth of knowledge."

Now, I am really confused. "Keeper, are you inferring the Holy Grail?"

"No, I ask that you only seek the peace and serenity of a new life with your companion. You must now take a seat in the space chairs and buckle yourselves in.

Both of you will be reprogrammed and then beamed to a distant galaxy one hundred light-years near Galaxy Fourteen."

All this was overwhelming to both of us. Before entering the space chairs, I asked him, "What are the alternatives of going back near my home-based solar system in Galaxy Fourteen?"

A pause followed and the keeper looked at us in a puzzled state. He replied, "I could give you a spaceship with a lifetime of fuel, food, air, and protection to travel through the endless cosmos in search of new life."

I asked, "What if we decide to leave the same way as we entered the cave?"

"Look out of the room into the cave, and tell me what you see," he said.

Complete darkness—a total black emptiness of space! Maybe all this was a dream—a concoction unreal and stimulating but desirable. Our minds were confused, and the answer to our situation seemed cloudy.

We waited as moments seemed to pass by like seconds on a clock. All we continued to see was darkness. I glanced over at Lambda Photon, and she seemed somewhat taken aback, as if there was a real entity walking toward us out of the darkness. She looked spellbound for an instant.

I then took my eyes off her and looked once again into the darkness. Still I saw nothing. I asked Lambda Photon, "What's wrong? Is it something with which we should be concerned?"

Still no reply came from her lips. I began to experience a cold, chilly feeling running through my body. Just then, a glowing white form emerged from the darkness and looked directly at us. The figure appeared to be a spaceman with his right hand and arm pointing toward us. Our eyes were fixed directly on him. I immediately felt a warm sensation pass through my body as if everything were okay and I should not fear this unusual chance meeting with the alien figure.

The white-clothed figure removed his space helmet visor and smiled. He didn't look familiar to me, but Lambda Photon seemed to embrace his thought wave transmission. Immediately, she spoke to the keeper, "Can you be real, or is this only a transcendental thought derived from my brain?"

Seconds flicked by with rapidity. The keeper looked at me and said, "Kit, this young man is your companion's brother, who has traveled through another time dimension trying to convey a message to her."

He then directed his attention toward Lambda Photon and said, "Young lady, you need to listen carefully to what your brother is about to ask you."

"Lambda Photon, are you okay? Do you love Kit so completely that you want to stay with him forever?"

"Yes, I'm fine, and I do love Kit with all my heart. He is a wonderful companion and soul mate."

"Lambda Photon, I just want you to know that it is our father's intent to move our planet from its present position in orbit around their respective star as to camouflage debris from outer space. This is an ingenious type of space warfare. Preparations are currently underway to take another planet and replace it in its position in space, thus preventing decomposition of life in modern-day Atlantis, thereby confusing the enemy."

"Sister, I just want you to know there are growing concerns about the increase of plasma bombarding the atmosphere of the New Empire. Mother and Daddy are worried about you and Kit."

"Oh, please tell them not to worry. We'll be fine. Brother, I relinquish all my rights to you. In the event of our parents' death, you will then become the ruler of the planet. I realize I may never see you again. Kit and I are getting married and going forward in time. Peace and happiness be with you and my family forever."

"Lambda Photon, you realize we may never see one another again."

"Yes, brother, I trust that all of you can accept my decision and wish the best for Kit and me."

With a salutary good-bye and best wishes for a happy and successful life, his image then faded and total darkness descended upon us.

Lambda Photon's thought-wave transmissions easily zeroed in on my thoughts with lightning-quick speed that would baffle a computer of the Lambda Four Alpha Series. Her main concern was for our safety and welfare. Our destiny seemed to lie directly before us. What should we do?

I was not one to make rash decisions. Rather, I realized this situation superseded many of the harrowing experiences we had already observed. I thought it odd that a mind probe could easily receive one's thought-wave transmissions and beam into a specific frequency. I had used that device to zero in on events affecting only the past, present, or future. I wondered how Lambda Photon and I could alter one or all of these. It didn't seem humanly possible that we could change the degree or present course of life.

My thoughts seemed tangled and embroidered in some great body yet unrevealed to us in our search for the way, the truth, and the life. I studied our situation from all points of view and decided to discuss it with Lambda Photon.

"Please tell me if there are any reasons you would like to return to your parents' time period."

"No, Kit, I will miss all of them, but my life is now with you, and I am willing to continue with our journey into the future."

I knew that once I told the keeper our decision to continue, our plans would be final. The trajectory would be laid, and we would be hurdled into the unknown. The keeper asked, "Have you reached your decision as to what you plan to do?"

I looked into his eyes and asked him, "Are you God?"

The keeper answered with these words, "I am that I am."

I knew at that moment he was the God I prayed to from my youth until now.

"Lambda Photon, I want you to meet God. He knows everything about us—our past successes and our failures. He also knows of our dreams."

She just stood there and looked at him. I knew she was trying to absorb all that was transpiring.

"Sweetheart, this is a monumental occasion in our lives, being in the presence of God and getting to speak with him."

"God, I have a very special request," said Kit.

"What is that, my son?"

"Would you honor and bless our marriage by performing our ceremony?"

"Yes, Kit. I know you both love each other and have already pledged your life to one another therefore, in as much as you have both agreed to love, honor, cherish, and obey, you are now pronounced husband and wife. My only requirement is that the two of you must always follow in the ways that lead to life eternal. You may now kiss the bride!"

There is no greater honor than to have God marry us.

"Kit, when you told me all about God, it was hard to imagine only one deity instead of four or five. Now I am beginning to understand how and why we have gotten to this place. This is a great honor for me likewise."

"We are now ready to go forward in time. Lambda Photon, are you ready to buckle in and be programmed?" I asked.

"Yes, Kit. I'm ready."

The keeper said, "Remember that once the trajectory is programmed, there will be no turning back."

We both nodded our heads and said, "Thank you."

The keeper's last instruction was for us to sit very still in the chairs and not to move regardless of the change in environment.

A whirling sound emerged and at once the cave disappeared and a new setting engulfed us. We found ourselves inside what appeared to be an ice cave. We were even dressed in warm, fur-lined clothing with a space-viewer over our heads to protect us from the icy chill of the meticulously formed and brightly illuminated rooms.

We got out of the chairs and stood up. All at once, the chairs disappeared into thin air, as if they never really existed. We walked through the ice palace and observed the richly formed stalagmites and stalactites. It was truly a beautiful work of art.

Suddenly, we came to a narrow room in the cave. It too was illuminated, and there were areas in it very much like bedrooms with sliding doors covering the entrance of each room. The doors seemed a bit warped and required manual dexterity to open them. I pushed hard with my hands and managed to open one door partially.

We walked in slowly and observed a warm module. Everything in the room looked like it had been left perfectly in place just for our inspection. There was even clothing in the drawers and pictures were hanging on the walls. We looked at all the objects and realized we had once again found a suitable home for the two of us. We had traveled so far. *I wonder what else the future has in store for us?*

Lambda Photon sat down on the bed and removed her space viewer from her eyes and the fur cap covering her head. She shook her hair briskly and lay back on the bed. I took off my space viewer and observed all the artifacts of the room. Somehow all these things seemed remotely familiar, but I couldn't explain why.

The décor of the room was well designed and complimented our personalities. Being curious, I scanned the room for something to recall from my memory bank to see if I had somehow been programmed to experience the subtleties of this life in the future.

The room was colorful with pictures of the countryside that were very unfamiliar to me, possibly derived from an alien planet. I looked cautiously at the objects in the room. Lambda Photon seemed content to rest awhile.

My thoughts seemed to project beyond my actions. There were things I wanted to say about what I saw in the room, but my brain was working ahead of my subconscious, absorbing and recording data that seemed to match things in the history of my life. I tried to remain perfectly at ease as thought impulses reverberated through my brain with the agility of an Olympian. I continued to scan the room but could not find anything connected to my past.

I then decided to walk out and observe a few of the other rooms. As I left, I noticed that Lambda Photon had fallen asleep. I walked down the corridor a scant two yards when I came upon another room. I placed my hand over the door monitor and couldn't believe my eyes. The room looked identical to my module in Galaxy Fourteen, even to the clothing in the chest of drawers. The figurines I once owned were still sitting on the cornice above my televiewer that I used as a telephone to communicate with friends.

I walked over to my bed. I guessed it was my bed; I really wasn't sure at that point what to believe. My subconscious began an immediate interrogation. *Can this be my room in Galaxy Fourteen? It is so familiar.* As I looked out the window, I realized this really was Galaxy Fourteen but almost ten to fifteen centuries later. What I was accustomed to had undergone an ice age; there were no signs of life anywhere. It seemed, for the moment, that we were the only two people alive. I hurried out of the room to confront Lambda Photon with the news.

Upon entering the room, I came to an abrupt halt. She was sitting on the bed holding some type of mechanical device that monitored communication land-to-land or laser-to-space. I tried to step backward through the entrance but encountered the force field. I was then jolted and thrust back into the room. I fell to the floor and then got up cautiously. "Lambda Photon, do you always carry scientific instruments like that around with you?"

She replied, "A woman must always be prepared to protect herself!"

"Sweetheart, I need you to remove the force field, as I have some startling news for you."

"I've turned it off, Kit. What's so important?"

"We've been sent back to my home in Galaxy Fourteen many centuries into the future."

"What! I can't believe it! Are you surprised or did you anticipate this happening to us, Kit?"

"Yes, I'm very surprised."

She then said, "I had a feeling this might happen. You seemed to want to return home in your search for the mysteries and complexities of life. Perhaps you shall now fulfill your destiny in your galaxy."

That statement began to echo in my consciousness as I looked into her loving eyes. The encompassing thoughts of the two of us being the only people left alive revealed puzzling and judgmental decisions regarding the success of our life together on this planet. We had finally met our fate.

Returning Home

I tried to keep my mind attuned to the reality that I had reached my home, even though it was centuries later. Inwardly, I felt that since everything materially was the same, I suppose I half-expected to find people just as when I lived in Galaxy Fourteen.

I turned to face Lambda Photon. Without saying a word, she read my thoughts and ideas of action that could result in complete transition and harmony on this planet for the two of us to survive. I guess I started to speak, but before I could say a word, she placed her hand over my mouth and said, "I understand your confusion and desire. We shall overcome the transition."

"Lambda Photon, we need to start walking to the Central Intelligence Headquarters and see if it is intact. Maybe the computer memory banks are still functional. If the power is low, we can use the electronic force field device to boost the needed power. My only hope is that we will be able to find out what happened to all the people and what has transpired on Galaxy Fourteen over the past centuries."

We walked toward the end of the module labeled Level Two. I pressed the admittance key that triggered a green light to come on. Instantly, a door opened, and we proceeded down a dimly lit corridor marked identically the same as when I had lived there. Somehow I knew from my memory bank that little had changed over the centuries to this particular level in the module.

As we reached Level Three, there was an admittance key, but this time as I triggered the key, a voice command was required. Seconds passed as I spoke our names, and the door opened automatically. We went into another corridor where a green light was flashing on and off in the median position of the hall. I missed the hustle and bustle of attendants, scientists, and space enthusiasts crowding the narrow hallway as I had so often moved from one room to another.

"Kit, why are these rooms coded mathematically?"

"The rooms were arranged so that the lower ones in number were closer to the opening of the building. I don't know why that plan was devised."

"Oh, Kit, look. What is that glass case?"

"When I lived here, schedules and records were often posted daily."

"Then why are these schedules encased in hard acrylic glass indicating the final departures from this planet? Just look at the date. It's inscribed AD 2850. Can you imagine? That's over eleven centuries ago. It's now AD 4000."

"I know, sweetheart. You have to remember that paper is now nonexistent. Everything is either electronic or computerized."

I found many things to be unbelievable. The walls looked relatively new, and the labels were clean and marked explicitly. I found it difficult to accept there was no visible evidence of people anywhere.

Lambda Photon insisted we move on down the corridor. I knew that to enter this area my voice monitor was needed for verification. Also, I had to remember my assignment code number. I thought for a moment and triggered the admittance key. I knew if I forgot the order of the code sequence and entered the Level Four area forcibly, we might be killed by the secret monitor installed as protector in this area.

Carefully, I pressed the admittance key and spoke the following sequence: *KBJ17427SE*. The door opened and we went inside. I couldn't believe this unit was still operational after all these centuries.

"Lambda Photon, I'm sorry I had to pull your hand so hard when we entered the room, but I knew the door monitor was protected by cross-beam lasers, and we only had a few seconds to get past those."

"That's okay. I understand."

As we entered the level, the lasers over the admittance door became functional. "Kit, are there any other monitoring devices located in the area that I should know about?"

"No, but stay close beside me, and do whatever I ask, and you will be safe."

The room was brightly lit by the computer monitors flashing on and off automatically, almost to the point of involuntary action.

"Kit, I've never seen computer monitors so scientifically advanced. And to think they were constructed many centuries ago."

"Lambda Photon, everything in this complex will continue to operate for another three thousand one hundred fifty years, provided the building is not destroyed. The power is atomic and stored one hundred meters below the building encased in lead to shield it from radioactivity. Since the planet was abandoned, the power has not been turned off. Any space traveler landing here would be able to obtain data needed for survival."

As we approached a large televiewer, we observed a film screen used to monitor space communication and store data of events that were purposely filmed for research, documentation, education, and leisure. I felt that some of the computer tapes held the key to the disappearance of human life on this planet.

My predictions could never have been more exact. The tapes were sequentially stored as before and dated—the last date being AD 2850. Could this have been the final recorded date of civilization? I wondered what happened to all the people.

As I walked over to the master computer and visually scanned the control buttons, I knew I must use meticulous care in operating the central control knobs. A wrong turn could set off an alarm that meant deadly complications for the two of us inside this chamber. I also knew these units had a fail-safe mechanism built into them to prevent sabotage.

My eyes scanned the mechanical buttons and automatic adjustments that were used to compensate for in-depth space technology in the preparation for storage data on long-range space missions. I took my eyes away for a brief moment and looked at Lambda Photon. She was listening to my thoughts as the nerve impulses moved through my brain as to the manipulation of the computer banks.

Immediately, I felt sensory stimuli penetrating the cerebrum conveying that Lambda Photon had experience working in the area of computer technology. An involuntary reflex then took place as I motioned her with the wave of my hand to assume command of the master computer. As I stepped back and relinquished the commands to her, I felt completely safe and at ease.

Lambda Photon withdrew the metallic device from her pocket and turned on the light switch as she moved it over the control panel without ever touching it.

"Wow, that is amazing! How did you do that?" I asked.

"Kit, whenever a light goes out on my electronic device over a control knob, that particular button is used for a computer memory scan. The device is very complicated, but extremely useful."

"I'm impressed."

Her technique took only about two minutes to locate and prescribe the sequential order of use for the computer scan. I was somewhat baffled by her adeptness and the precision by which she operated the memory scan computer. I prayed she would not accidentally hit the attack computer button. If that happened, I wasn't completely sure that we would ever be allowed to leave this level again without pre-emptive gunfire from unknown ports of entry in the room used for protection against alien saboteurs or advancing armies.

Fortunately, we did not encounter any problems in determining the computer sequence. I couldn't recall my galaxy ever being at war with any foreign civilization.

I guess as Lambda Photon turned toward me, she mentally projected the message that everything is ready for computer activation.

I stepped forward and observed her as she moved toward the solution of the prime directive—the present people of Galaxy Fourteen. I looked with anticipation as the whirl of control knobs moved clockwise and counterclockwise with equal rapidity.

High-pitched sounds were then emitted by the computer as the memory scans were revitalized and reprogrammed toward the solution of the problem—"What happened to the people?"

My curiosity was increasing moment-by-moment as computer tapes all across the room moved with quick jerks and spins. After about five minutes, Lambda Photon said, "We are now ready to see on the televiewer what happened to the populace of the world you loved in Galaxy Fourteen?"

As seconds ticked by, I imagined certain unbelievable things that could have happened such as:

1. Time warp

2. Inevitable disaster

3. Uncontrollable viral attack on the known population in the galaxy

4. Intergalactic war using invisible gas to neutralize all the inhabitants, even down to the holocaust—total destruction of all life

5. Habitation of the underworld of this planet

6. Meteoric destruction of the surface world by the solar wind of the nearest star

7. Orbit decay from our existence in space

8. A self-destruct mechanism based on computer research determined by food needs of the living

population—famine causing mercy-killing

9. Self-disintegrators caused by environmental mental illness moving as a wave phenomenon over the surface area of the entire galaxy.

I fantasized all kinds of ideas for the loss of human life. I was thankful, however, for the operation of the control computers in Level 4.

Lambda Photon realized that I was daydreaming and said, "Kit, pay attention!"

I realized where my thoughts were leading me, so I directed my attention to the televiewer. Waves of static covered the screen, and then a picture image focused on the monitor outlining human figures moving through a modern city of the twenty-eighth century.

I was so fascinated by the architecture that my eyes hastily absorbed the environment and its mode of life. There appeared to be no relevant degree of implication to defend against loss of life. The picture then crossed lines to a scene from the governors of this galaxy. Their words serenaded the fact of human survival here as well as on the outer planets.

The governors were concerned that so many people had decided to migrate to the free lands of the outer ring of planets several light-years away. They also realized that since fewer people remained, the populace could not sustain its lifestyle as it had in the past.

The outer ring of planets offered inhabitants opportunities for a new lifestyle, adventure, colonization, leadership, government, an escape from the working world, exploration, freedom of speech and worship, and identification of a new way of life.

All leaders were afraid the people would regress to their former, but primitive, ways of life. Simply stated, they wouldn't be like pioneers, but colonists in a new world, free to exercise what limited authority they had learned from their previous life. They were afraid the present civilization would become only a dormant niche in the branches of time.

Apparently, the leaders of their world realized the urgency of the government. They decided everyone should leave together. Scientifically, it would have been dangerous to perform a shutdown procedure using an atomic element with a large decay rate. A decision was made to leave the computers functional to inform future space travelers of their whereabouts in the event that communication necessitated immediate survival by their people. At least they wouldn't be totally lost on this planet.

It was believed that if the computers were properly controlled and monitored, space travelers could efficiently set up shop with minimal difficulty and eventually unite with the outer ring of planets. After all, the computers were operated by nuclear energy, having half-lives in excess of three to five thousand years, long enough for future space travelers to make telecommunication or teleportation by their method of travel.

I was only 1,200 years late; not bad for a young space engineer.

Lambda Photon queried about my facial gestures as I observed the televiewer with empathy and speculation. My thoughts seemed to go in other directions as I observed the last remnants of human life leaving the land I loved in my youth and manhood. I tried not to show emotion and dismay at the realization of our fate. I knew that the two of us would have to employ all the technological training we shared to survive in our present environment.

I found Control Level 4 somewhat baffling because it was in such excellent working condition even though the human factor had been gone for some time. When I walked into a clean and immaculate room, I expected human hands to have had a part in it. Not so in this case.

Through viewing the tapes, we found the computer era had programmed service robots that cleaned the entire area and humidified it to the precise oxygen content levels appropriate for survival should human life ever return. There appeared to be all kinds of backup units to modify and compensate for modular readouts across the enlarged space board, recording all trips by space travelers throughout the galaxy.

Galaxy Fourteen was very similar to the New Empire. I was eager to inquire of the human factor through the stored memory of the computer 4 alpha. Lambda Photon programmed the computer for the presence of human extraterrestrial life on this quadrant, and the computer printed out the predictability of human life in our segment of space was one in one trillion.

For the time being, other human life seemed a remote improbability. The aloneness seemed to take hold of us as we tried to explore all the vistas that the computer could offer in the way of survival. We had met our fate and accepted it. The realm of life would now begin to form anew as we rekindled a new spirit of life.

Realizing our immediate situation, we agreed that a computer scan of the planet's surface would perhaps enlighten us as to the resources available for survival in different sectors of this planet. This time Lambda Photon programmed the computer according to the nearest cities, and the televiewer lit up. Tapes of the people living there showed the cities under human control.

Our scan of the four nearest cities revealed an abundant supply of space food capsules and water. Medicinal drugs seemed of little value since our bodies had been injected at birth with Neotraxin to prevent invading viruses and bacterial infections for at least one hundred years of normal human life.

The transportation vacuum tubes still appeared functional and valuable. Also, the communication devices were intact and in a safe clearance location. Weapon arsenals in each city still had sufficient ammunition to secure the planet. Together, Lambda Photon and I felt that we could maintain control on this planet and live in harmony with the environment. Our attachment and dependence on each other seemed impenetrable as we searched for our destiny. We decided that the Level 4 computers had fulfilled our needs, and we left the area for some rest.

We traveled through a series of sliding doors and long corridors until we came to the area where we first found ourselves. I felt sure this area somehow held the key to life itself. My austerity and will to survive zoomed. It seemed as though the libido of my mind and the central nervous system were in total harmony as to the proper sequences I was to follow in the days ahead. New avenues of life lay ahead for our future. I could not help but wonder if this were a dream or reality? Time, it seemed, would conquer all.

We went into my module and lay down to rest. The twilight of consciousness had surpassed the conscious world and projected us into a few hours of much-needed sleep.

Separation

As my mind began to dream, it seemed for the moment that my double life had taken its identity into the dream world. I observed once again my exploration of the New Empire. Many friends had been made there. The libido of my mind seemed to be reprogramming itself for a new and more sophisticated experience, perhaps unknown to the conscious mind.

In my dream world, I hastened to experience the new era of sensation that awaited me. I watched and listened eagerly. Coming through a doorway into the corridor was Lambda Photon asking, "Can you believe that we are meeting here in a microcosm of inner space in your dream?"

The subject was very enlightening and quite profound. I had always projected the idea of two minds joining in complete harmony in the phantasm of dreams. Yet, here we were, totally linked through transference of the libido interchange. Each of us was dreaming and seeing the other in the same dream.

I thought we were in suspended animation through a time lock of the libido-transference mind-link, phenomena only conjectured by scientists centuries before in the realms of astrological circles. The fact that each of us could see the other and talk without using extrasensory perception made the dream much more realistic.

In my subconscious, I knew the mind-link had been accomplished successfully. Perhaps it was for the libido to show its unpredicted strength and ability. These ideas were both stimulating and intrinsically refreshing. I eagerly awaited the next turn of events.

"Sweetheart, this is a perfect meeting of the minds. We can feel safe and free of the ills of the world around us. Uniting our minds into a congruent pattern, there is probably nothing we cannot accomplish."

We felt we had crossed over the barrier where people say they use only ten percent of the brain's total capacity. In fact, we had doubled our capacity for productive use.

I began to experience sensations of the body and mind. To discover and render the use of one's soul in the unconscious state while still alive seemed too vast for words. I found that I could walk, run, jump, and carry on melodic and diverse conversations without the least bit of guilt or dismay of my partner exploding at me with precarious and temperamental tantrums. It was certainly a dream world come true—a definite escape from reality!

I knew it could not last forever and that we would have to return to the real world of consciousness. The thrill of adventure lay in the doorway of dreamland. We clamored through the door toward our next rendezvous of unconsciousness with anticipation and glee.

The light of our dreams would be the torch of our salvation in the real world of Galaxy Fourteen. There lay the truth. The science of astral projection somehow had become the most omnipotent factor in shaping the destiny of our lives. We anticipated the next event.

I cannot begin to relate the earth-shaking ideas and mind-challenging theories that traveled through the central nervous system of our bodies. I fantasized phenomena happening to us, events never thought of by modern man. As long as we remained in the unconscious state, our souls were free to experience the ultimate sensations of pleasure and pain. It was like leading a double life in two different worlds.

The world of sleep combined with our successful mind-link opened new horizons yet uncharted for the two of us. The sunset of Galaxy Fourteen in comparison to the unconscious state represented a brief look into the twilight zone where no laws were barred and conscious sensations were uncensored. Avenues of pleasure and displeasure circumnavigated the whole of our conscious and unconscious thought patterns.

Every occurrence in a dream could now be traced to ancestral figures projected through our genes or chromosomes in perfect link with the brain.

Our patterns of thought had been conditioned through learning experiences from birth to the present. However, through the mind-link we were now able to tap uncharted areas of the brain and to see figuratively things from our past that perhaps had affected our lives countless centuries before our present life. The linking of our minds had now transferred an aura of energy designed to investigate and experience a discovery of areas totally in the dream world.

Literally, in an unconscious, sleep-like state, we were able to see history relived and rekindled through the eyes of other people and their happenings, just as they occurred. I was now beginning to train my thoughts on the ultimate problem—the destiny of my life with Lambda Photon.

The world we lived in seemed like home, but was it really? Was everything I experienced actually a dream that happened in suspended animation aboard a spaceship destined for a journey to the end of time? The libido seemed totally in control as thoughts whisked by at light speed. Whether the conscious or unconscious world was there, the ominous presence of tomorrow seemed harmonious with the spirits of our bodies.

The mind-link was the ultimate escape from the realities of today or yesterday. To predispose the combined transference of thought wave patterns into a single unit consisting of dreams represented man's final conquest of the inner self. Though tranquil in thought, being at peace with oneself represented pure happiness. Even though our lifestyle was somewhat different back home in Galaxy Fourteen, the mind-link set everything straight in the newness of the real world we faced in our everyday occurrences and experiences as we explored this planet.

I had been awake for a short time when I sat up in the bed and looked around the room. Lambda Photon was still fast asleep. I did not want to awaken her as she might sense my concern for our survival. I decided to walk down the hallway to another room looking for clues to my lost identity.

Once inside the room, I walked over to a desk and pulled out the top drawer. It was just as I expected.

The junk drawer still contained all the trinkets I had collected from youth. As I examined the contents, my brain seemed to regress to those yesteryears. My good luck piece, an ancient Egyptian gold coin with the Sphinx on one side and Ra, the sun god, on the other, was intact.

The coin was supposed to protect the bearer from all curses and spells. I picked it up and squeezed it firmly. I could feel the surge of blood in the capillaries of my hand. There was something special about the coin that always fascinated me. I wondered if it possessed magical powers beyond the scope of my predecessors back in the beginning on Earth.

Perhaps the fact that I was the protector of the coin awarded me gifted talents which guided me toward the city of Atlantis in the distant future.

I began to reflect on all my experiences in the New Empire. As I was studying the gold coin, sunlight streamed through an opening in the window of the module and struck the side with the sun god on it. The coin appeared vitreous and fiery as sun drops danced on its shield. I almost thought the coin would change its identity and fall to the floor just as liquid mercury would if moved the least bit. Instead, the light striking it was diffused and refracted toward one of the walls.

At once, a holographic image appeared in ghostly form. I was so spellbound that I didn't move or try to run away. A Greek warrior dressed in bright gold metal sheathed about his body appeared directly in front of me. He was wearing a gold-crested helmet and had a warm and handsome face with blue eyes, a straight nose, and an indented chin. He stood approximately six feet tall. Hanging at his side next to a scroll bound to his garments was a fiery gold sword. On his feet were boots of gold. All his garments glowed, just like the coin.

He spoke not a word as he studied me from head to toe. Taking his right hand, he carefully removed the scroll from his garments, and a fireball sent the scroll from his hand to mine. Frankly, I was impressed with the uniqueness of such a meeting. The image spoke not a word but moved his hands in such a way that I knew I should open the scroll and observe its meticulously conceived transcript with care.

Slowly removing the binding, I opened the scroll and began to piece the meaning of the document together. As I began to decipher its context intermittently, I frequently looked up to see what the image was doing. He was smiling at me, and the glitter of his teeth was like drops of whitest snow. As I perused the scroll, some of the signs and symbols were unfamiliar, but slowly I began to decipher pieces of the puzzle.

I was looking at one of the greatest and most famous rulers of Mesopotamia and Europe. The splendor and awesome majesty of him enthralled me and manifested his worthiness as a warrior and defender of the realm of his empire.

A shock wave thundered through me as I realized I was looking at the handsome form of Alexander the Great. He was everything I had ever read about or discussed in my early schooling. I wondered why I was the lucky one chosen to meet the most famous man of his day. As the sunlight veered off the coin, the image disintegrated, leaving only the scroll in my hand to observe and scrutinize. *In the next moment, destiny may lie in my hands.*

I could not actually discern the degree of understanding I had experienced. Perhaps this was only a one-in-a-million chance meeting with a god-like figure whom I idolized. Joy seeped within every portal of my inner being as I realized I had uncovered yet another truth in the mysteries of life.

Again I took the gold coin and turned it over in my hand. As I glanced at it passionately, I wondered what other knowledge might be dissected by the use of sunlight striking it. I visualized all sorts of preconceived ideas about what knowledge would be revealed if I turned it at odd angles to the sun.

Would my surprise visitor return as gloriously as before? Maybe next time there would be no image. I was too undaunted to believe that I would be shortchanged at seeing Alexander the Great once again. I knew I had experienced a rare privilege in seeing him and reading the inscribed document he sent to me. I wondered if I should awaken Lambda Photon and tell her the strange news of my most recent discovery as she was keenly aware of my abilities as a scientist and adventurer.

I decided to leave well enough alone and investigate other artifacts of the junk drawer. Only this time I kept the gold coin in my pocket. Looking again in the drawer, I gazed upon my toy space gun that looked so authentic. As a boy I had imagined myself a space liberator of galaxies and star systems.

On the pretense of playing space hero, I instinctively picked up the toy space gun and fired it toward the sunlit window. Strangely, energy appeared to be emitted from the somewhat aged gun and shattered the window. I was thunderstruck by the awesome power that was exhibited by my primitive space gun.

Releasing my grip from the gun, I set it on the chest. I was somewhat shaken and perplexed as to what I had just observed. Maybe I had imagined the gun firing. I looked down the hallway and realized that Lambda Photon must still be asleep. Surely she would have heard the sounds of the bursting windowpane and awakened. The proof lay therein.

The toy gun had actually fired energy, not air. Picking it up again, I fired it with simultaneous bursts. This time I only heard *click-click*. No energy was emitted. Did energy leave the gun because I commanded from my inner self a release of subliminal power to be administered from my being toward the window? Was telekinesis partially responsible?

I racked my brain for a logical answer. I even looked for signs of forced entry in the toy space gun. However, it looked the same as it had 1,200 years ago. Only slight wear accompanied the outer finish of the gun.

I placed it back into the drawer, still not satisfied with what I had witnessed. The sheer fact that for once in the turn of a century, power had escaped from the unpractical to the real world both alarmed and bewildered me. What did the future hold on this planet?

Again I looked into the mixed up drawer at the things only a young child would collect. I had once captured a beautiful Monarch butterfly. As I opened the box and looked at the precious specimen, a twist of fate occurred. The butterfly's wings seemed to return to the beauty of life once again.

My heart was filled with compassion just as a small child would feel for a loved one or a pet. For an inkling of time, the butterfly fluttered its wings and flew about the room, darting to and fro, before once again settling in the box it had graced for so long.

I studied it for a few moments although it didn't move again. My heart pounded for answers my brain couldn't translate. I had become as curious as life itself. Placing the lid back on the box, I laid it beside the toy space gun. I didn't realize at the time that the exploration of my past had given me the fulfillment of the future.

I had an unusual feeling that the scroll I had received earlier had something to do with all these strange phenomena. Somehow, a newly conceived power seemed to be tied to me through the time-space sequence of my thought-wave patterns, transfixed from birth to now through the transference of the scroll to me. Having both touched the scroll and read its contents seemingly gave me new life, a feeling I had longed for inwardly over the decades. One would not think that a mere scroll would affect a person's mind, however, it did.

Again I looked into the drawer at other intimate and personal belongings. There lay a wooden box with two hinges on the back. I had carved a rosebud on the top when I was young and even painted it for preservation.

My mind began to question what uncertain power lay mysteriously in the little box? Would the sins of the world escape from the box as in the mythical story of Pandora?

I picked up the box and placed it on top of the chest. It still looked just as beautiful as when I had first carved it. I silently studied the box for a moment, and a thought entered my mind. *Why not give it to Lambda Photon? After all, this will be a personal gift, and surely she'll accept it graciously.*

All at once, I felt a strong urge to touch the rose on the box. The electricity that seemed to flow between my hand and the box took on tangible realism. Instantaneously, the box began to glow and a real, perfect rose was transfixed onto my hand from the box. There had been no sound emitted by the occurrence although the aroma of the flower was present. Within seconds, the rose left my hand and returned to its same position on the box.

It was strange that with all my movement Lambda Photon had not awakened. This puzzled me but didn't alarm me at the time. I picked up the little wooden box and decided to return it to the drawer with uncertainty. This strange power of the box had greatly confused and bewildered me. Frankly, I was astonished by all I had seen. I yearned to learn more of the mysteries of the drawer.

The secrets of my past had been dormant for years. Why were they surfacing now as a key to my survival? I also saw toy marbles I had won as a boy. I picked up the pint-size jar of marbles and set them on top of the chest. The light piercing the window gave a glistening effect to them. I stepped back as the marbles seemed to radiate their own energy. The entire room was illuminated by the power of the pint-size jar, and I was spellbound by its mystic powers. At that point I decided to go check on Lambda Photon.

As I returned to the room, I took the jar of marbles with me. The brightness seemed to leave the jar and move through the room under its own power, totally independent of the sunlight striking it. Random movement of light scattered about the room hovering over Lambda Photon as if poised for some special function. In a matter of seconds, the light returned to the jar and the brightness dissipated, leaving the jar of marbles reflecting only sunlight. What significance did the aura of bright light have in leaving the jar and hovering over Lambda Photon?

Was I witnessing a real entity composed of a psychokinetic touch from my hand being guided by my subconscious mind? Bolts of high-speed intellectual gibberish found their way into my brain as it tried to sort out some type of recognizable fact.

Lambda Photon awakened and I asked her, "Will you go with me? I want you to observe what I have found."

"Sure," she replied.

We looked at postcards of places I had been and others from relatives and friends. I guess they reminded me of the wonderful times I had had as a boy.

We looked in the drawer and found my identification cards. I wondered why I'd kept them.

"Darling, please understand that I am not a junk collector. I just like old things, and as I was growing up, I purchased some things like these old fountain pens and used ink cartridges for writing by hand. Of course, they were not used in my lifetime, but I always enjoyed studying about ancient civilizations and how we became so technologically advanced. These items serve as a reminder of what our ancestors had to do to accomplish such a menial task as writing documents."

Next to them lay a piece of symbolism very special to me, the picture of a heart with a cross piercing it. I was told as a youth that it had belonged to my grandmother; therefore, I had always revered it and kept it safe. It had no monetary value, yet even as I picked it up, I felt a burning sensation pass over my forehead, and I wiped the sweat cleanly from my face. As I looked at the heart again, the image cast by the heart and cross seemed to take on a new meaning, almost resembling that of my life.

"Kit, I can't believe all your things from childhood are still here."

"Neither can I, Lambda Photon."

At that moment a thought permeated my brain. *I have the heart to bear my cross in this life as a futuristic time traveler despite inevitable difficulties.* That idea seemed to grasp my being as I turned and looked into the mirror. My whole body now glowed as I held the picture firmly in my hand.

A newness of purpose eluded me as I turned and placed the picture back into its respective place in the drawer. Time had been good to me up to now and the illusion or disillusion I expected seemed to shake the horizon of the mind as I awaited the next sequence of events.

For some reason, I turned from the chest, walked past Lambda Photon, and approached the entrance to the room. I examined the entrance to see if there were any new or old wall panels still in use. Surprisingly, the old locks still lay in place behind the wall.

Taking out my knife, I carefully unscrewed the lock on the left side of the entrance and removed the outer facing. In a little plastic box lay one of my most intrinsic treasures—a gold bracelet that my parents had placed on my arm when I was only one or two years old. I was afraid I would lose this possession, so I carefully hid it in the most inconspicuous place I could find. It wasn't so much a monetary treasure as a symbol that I had parents who loved me.

I experienced a warm feeling as I took the little box into my hands that held the gold bracelet. It looked so tiny and fragile. I then removed the bracelet and placed it in my pocket. I had a feeling as I did so that all would be well in the days ahead.

I was growing tired, so Lambda Photon suggested I lie down on the bed and rest. Instantly, I fell asleep.

The End of Time

I awakened hours later by the prodding of Lambda Photon. As I sat up and looked into her beautiful, young face, I read her thoughts instinctively and realized that everything was not as perfect as it seemed. I don't think she felt insecure; however, with my help, we would be able to face the future in a positive manner.

I was trying to discern any phenomena that might explain why these series of events were occurring, as I didn't want to alarm Lambda Photon. Perhaps she was not accustomed to places like this, or maybe she was using the libido of her mind for long-range scanning from foreign undetectable beings in the corridors of our new home.

Lambda Photon was gazing into space as her eyes locked into a complete stare. Her manner suggested there was something about which I should be concerned. For some strange reason, I walked over to the chest and picked up my toy space gun so as to protect us. She quickly read my thoughts and said, "What do you think you're going to do with that?"

I told her, "Watch and see this new power of mine."

She replied, "Do you think you can protect us with a toy gun?"

"Lambda Photon, many strange things have happened to us that it is impossible for me to explain. I'll just have to ask you to trust me."

"Kit, I do trust you, but quit fantasizing about your toy space gun. There is no way it can protect us! We need to check out the remainder of the modules."

"I agree with you. Let's proceed through the corridor."

So many things had happened to me while a passenger on the spaceship of time that I scarcely noticed the second hand on my watch was spinning at a tremendous velocity, perhaps many miles per hour. I wondered how the tiny watch remained intact while this phenomenon was occurring. "Lambda Photon, wait just a minute. I need to stop for a moment and examine some data." Using this as an excuse, I checked out some of the things in my pockets and the walls of the corridor.

I observed the date on my watch, and it was changing at light speed. I did consider the fact that we could be in a time warp. *Will the door open to a place where time accelerates but the things in it remain perfectly stationary and somewhat transfixed?*

Lambda Photon used her highly developed extrasensory perception skills and shared my confusion. She said, "The most important thing is that we are together."

The thought of being caught in time travel was something beyond my wildest dreams. I fantasized many phenomena as I looked at Lambda Photon. Our thoughts seemed locked together as we searched for a means of escape from our time portal. *Are we truly at the end of time? If we reach the final counterpart of time itself, is this the ultimate end of the universe for us?*

Our time portal had locked us in a planet equipped with everything we needed to survive. It was obvious we weren't aging, as we both looked young and full of life. Every experience was keyed to us in some way as if the great programmer of the universe had so destined us to experience all these phenomena in order.

We yearned to know and interpret the mysteries of life as we explored the cosmos of the future in a land saturated with the salt of the Earth. Uncalculated accuracy was something that I thought was reserved for machines, yet we had changed little in appearance. The temperature seemed normal, despite the erratic movement of the synchronisms of my watch. Also, the sun in the sky appeared in its natural position.

Then a thought-wave pattern crossed my mind. *Could we be increasing in time? Have I somehow, without knowing it, been able to unlock the acceleration mechanism for increasing time in its natural state?*

Could Lambda Photon and I have stumbled upon the mechanism for triggering the Fountain of Youth or has the great programmer in the sky deemed it appropriate for us to remain in his garden of Eden seemingly of our own accord and will? These thoughts seemed to illuminate all electrical energy in the libido of my mind as I looked down the periphery of the darkened corridor.

Could I willfully cause the corridor to increase in brightness? At that instant, Lambda Photon tuned in on the electrical stimulus of this thought pattern. An increase of energy seemed to bolt its way into my thought groupings as I sought clues to the odd occurrences we had experienced toward the end of time.

I desperately needed a plan to explain the phenomena. "Lambda Photon, we need to return to my module and perform the mind-link test. There may be danger in attempting to seek the end of eternity."

"Kit, what will happen to us if our bodies die while we are in the mind-link stream of unconsciousness?"

"Dear, our souls will remain joined together as an entity forever, even beyond time itself. Are you in agreement that this is what you want to do? You must be sure."

"Yes, Kit. Everything is fine. I never want to be separated from you, even in death."

"I can't be sure of that because everything is up to God. He created us and sent us here to accomplish his purpose for our lives."

It was a beautiful and unselfish idea, making her the perfect companion. We talked of all our journeys, visits, dreams, and aspirations in the world years ago. I was surprised that Lambda Photon liked to do the same things in her youth that I did. We shared many common joys.

"Dear, when I was a teenager, I dreamed of meeting a beautiful girl in distant space who would love and care about me. I was so busy in Galaxy Fourteen with my studies that I had little time to get to know members of the opposite sex. I did meet a few who were nice, but most of them were not interested in me personally. I mostly concentrated on my studies and entered the space academy when I got old enough."

"That is very enlightening, as I shared many of the same academic interests. My father and mother made sure their children were well educated and refined in the arts and sciences. Because they were so overprotective, I had little time to meet or date boys. My dream was to meet and fall in love with someone like you. God knew what he was doing when he brought us together."

I enjoyed hearing all her wonderful stories as well as telling her mine. When she seemed satisfied that each of us was ready to continue our mystical journey, she put her arms around me and hugged me. She asked, "Are you ready?"

"Yes!" I replied.

I knew the time had come to perform the mind-link. "Lambda Photon, we must lie down on the bed, join hands, and erase every thought from our conscious minds."

"Then let's get started."

I knew before the mind-link could become successful, the stream of consciousness would have to intertwine from the electrical energy outburst from each of the libidos of our minds in an unconscious state. Once achieved, the mind-link could thus utilize one entity—the combined total being of two people—and project our thought patterns into complete harmony toward the end of time itself.

As we lay there trying to clear our minds, I said, "Lambda Photon, I hope you realize that once we enter the mind-link, we might become entrapped at the site of the end of time and free-float in a world unknown in time and space. If that occurs, our entity might remain forever in a place much like the garden of Eden."

"Well, Kit, if that happens, we will just have to accept it."

Maybe this could be close to perfection or redemption for a world contrasted by war, disease, pestilence, and destruction. The destiny of man tomorrow lay just over the horizon in the unconscious world of thought.

Had we remembered a world created from the beginning and ending identically as creation had begun? We were on the threshold as we slowly closed our eyes and began to clear our minds of debris and worry. We had agreed before the experience that we would transfix our minds on the city of Atlantis so as to join in the realm of the cosmos.

Moments passed as I relaxed my hand with Lambda Photon's. One thought permeated my mind—*Atlantis! Atlantis!* Suddenly, I felt myself moving without a body in free fall toward the city of Atlantis. I was wearing a bright gold, silk outfit. As I approached the city, Lambda Photon appeared to be coming near me dressed similarly. We walked toward each other silently and joined hands. At once, a large bubble enclosed us and began moving parallel to the city. We continued past the city into the darkness of oblivion.

Our hands and minds were joined toward the ultimate conquest. Seconds ticked by, and then minutes seemed to erase themselves from the watch board of time. Our bright clothing illuminated the bubble as we continued moving through the final dimension. Time passed when I thought we were slowing down, but we continued uninterrupted.

The energy joining our beings inside the bubble was stimulating and refreshing in the newness of life eternal. I turned and looked at Lambda Photon.

"Oh darling, I wish I had a mirror so you could see your beautiful face."

"What is it, Kit?"

"Your face is so beautiful and shows no signs of aging."

"Oh my goodness! Kit, your face is glowing and you even look younger. Why is this happening to us?"

"I don't know. Maybe we'll understand as we complete the mind-link."

Raising my hand, I touched her cheek and rubbed it gently. I had an unusual feeling pass through my veins. She gripped my hand even more tightly, as if to reassure me of her love. Her eyes followed mine as a kind of joy and love passed from my eyes into hers.

Unspeakable communication enveloped as our thoughts became one, and we turned and forced the inevitable blackness of our voyage to the end of time. We peered into the darkness seeing nothing, knowing nothing, but expecting much.

Suddenly, the bubble began slowing down and eventually stopped. Anticipation grasped our very beings as we waited for the final answer concerning the mystery of the end of time.

Seconds ticked by. "Lambda Photon, hold me tightly. This must be the end of time." The world began in blackness and would end in blackness. Fear seemed far, far away. I thought silently for a moment. *There is a beginning and ending—right?* It would seem so by the logistics of natural phenomena.

We scanned our memory banks for data on the theory of burning Phlogiston. There had to be a source of all life-giving power in the universe, but for the moment we could not conceive of anything other than God who would be capable of being definitive in explaining natural phenomena.

By contrast, our bubble may have taken us to the limit of time, but our minds, linked perfectly together, seemed to transcend, even here in eternity. I half expected a bright blast of light to break our bubble and open new vistas of country sides, simply to comply with our needs as in the garden of Eden. But nothing seemed to happen in this remote place. Neither sound nor pictorial image occurred to increase our aptitude of inquiry into the unknown realm of our quiescent journey into this dimension.

We realized at this point of our voyage into time that in the beginning there was but one man and one woman. Out of the flesh came a populated world inhabiting many planets that were intrinsically moved to their surroundings by inverted time travel. We finally understood our place in time, and we lovingly embraced each other.

I felt my mind-link slipping away from Lambda Photon. Slowly, but surely, my entity began moving apart from her, as if each of us knew this was good-bye, a good-bye each resented to the point of hate and disillusionment. The mind-link was broken; I awakened, and my eyes slowly opened to see a strange and awkward sight.

∞

I was suddenly back aboard the spacecraft *Fanfare* on its journey to Butres Lettus, destination unknown, destination unexplored. A doctor in the medical unit screamed, "He's waking up from the coma!"

I felt confused as I looked at the doctor and all the other people gathering around me. I could hear a voice saying, "Lieutenant Bartusch, you are safe. Just lie still, and I will try to explain what has happened to you. When you laid down to rest on the mother ship three weeks ago before descending in the space hop, for some unknown reason, you became unconscious and lapsed into a deep coma. We have continually monitored your vital organs and given intravenous fluids and injections daily to keep you alive. During this time, you kept speaking of alien people and many times called out the name Lambda Photon."

That name Lambda Photon sounds familiar to me.

"Kit, how are you?" asked my best friend, Steve Matthews.

"Oh, Steve, I'm so glad to see you. What has happened to me?"

"From all the information I have been able to collect, it is apparent the mother ship's space hop you were supposed to board landed on the surface of the planet you were assigned to explore. Workers scanned for soil samples, studied mineralogy, conducted fuel studies, and explored possible space colonization from Galaxy Fourteen. There were no life forms or people found by the ships' sensors on the planet or any of the neighboring planets that were explored."

"Steve, I find that so hard to believe. Have you confirmed this information with Mission Control?"

"Yes, Kit. It's authentic, and everything has been documented."

"I know it sounds unreal, but I must tell you that I have had some very unusual things happen to me during this time. I experienced some type of phenomena that allowed me to believe I was traveling on the spacecraft while fulfilling my duties. During this time, I met aliens, experienced various types of time travel, met a beautiful girl named Lambda Photon, and fell in love. I also heard the voice of God telling both of us what to do, and he was the one who sent us back to Galaxy Fourteen in the year AD 4000."

"Kit, this is almost unbelievable! Did anything else happen to you that was unique?"

"Yes. Everything! One thing I noticed was that when I experienced excruciating pain in the temple area, I lost my eyesight. Also, on several occasions, I was moved to different locations without being aware of how I got there. Throughout all these episodes, Lambda Photon was my constant companion. I met her family members, who were descendants of the city of Atlantis. You would be amazed at the degree of technological advancements I was given the opportunity of observing. Please don't share this with anyone, as I don't understand any of it myself at this point in time. I hope you now understand my need to talk with Captain Vick."

I sat up groggily and stared at the people in total disbelief. I asked Steve, "Could you arrange for the captain to come see me? I have some urgent information that is confidential and extremely important to the space voyage."

"Kit, I'll go get him right now. While I'm gone, I want you to relax and let the medical staff examine you to determine if you have suffered any debilitating results from the three-week coma."

"Okay, Steve, but tell the captain to come immediately."

The ship's doctors and nurses checked me over physically and mentally.

"Nurse, that medicine smells awful. Do I have to drink that stuff?"

"Yes, I'm afraid you do, Lieutenant Bartusch. It will help relax you and provide us the opportunity to run necessary scans."

I still found it hard to believe that all these things had happened to me. As I lay there, I sought some type of clues to prove the things I had experienced were genuine. I reached in the pocket of my pants and felt the gold piece, my knife, and my gold bracelet. Now surely the captain knew that I didn't carry all those things around with me every day. In a moment, he arrived on the scene.

"At ease, Lieutenant Bartusch. There is no need to salute me."

I began to relate all the facts of my dream to him. Atlantis, the New Empire, Lambda Photon, and my journeys through time and space were some of the experiences I mentioned. He seemed fascinated and listened intently.

I finally asked him, "Do you think that all these things really could have happened to me although my body remained in a coma-like state aboard the spacecraft?"

He said, "We are not altogether sure what really happened to you. There were no medical causes as to why you passed out and remained in this unnatural state. I shall, for the record, place your transcript on file for future reference."

He then left the medical quarters. I didn't think

anyone believed me.

Steve, "Could I be dreaming this segment where I returned to the *Fanfare* unharmed and still be a science officer aboard a well-known spaceship?"

"Kit, I don't know. Tell me more about your experience."

I closed my eyes and slowly began an extensive recitation of the chain of events that had just occurred.

"Steve, believe me when I tell you that everything I've related to you and Captain Vick is the truth. I don't know how or why it happened, and I can't explain the objects found in my possession."

"Kit, I've never doubted you, as you have been a faithful friend throughout life."

"I appreciate your honesty, Steve, and the fact that you realize something has transpired with my body that is totally futuristic and beyond the realm of anything either of us can comprehend. I also want you to know I met a girl named Lambda Photon, fell in love, and actually traveled through time with her back to Galaxy Fourteen in AD 4000."

"Wow, Kit! That seems surreal."

"Steve, my one wish in life is to be reunited with her."

"Do you believe you will ever find her, Kit?"

"My hope is that whatever power caused me to experience these occurrences will return and send me back to her. Regardless of what happens, our friendship will be treasured forever."

If I could only return to the time portal with Lambda Photon, I would never complain again. There I would be well cared for and loved, and all my needs would be met. I wondered, *Does she miss me?*

"Kit, Kit! It's me, Steve. What's happening to you?"

Steve, Steve, Steve....

As if a massive chain reaction occurred, I felt myself picked up in a cyclonic storm and wrenched into another time portal. Perhaps God had listened to my prayers and was projecting me to the one I loved at the end of time.

∞

Suddenly, I was in a garden filled with lovely and exotic flowers. The newness of life seemed everywhere. I called out, "Lambda Photon! Are you here? If so, where are you?"

A voice replied, "I am here, my love."

We rushed toward each other exuberantly and enjoyed a kind of sharing never before experienced by modern man. Separation would no longer exist for us.

"Kit, I thought you were gone forever. I prayed to God and asked him to send you back to me. Being alone in the garden without you was traumatizing, and I felt so alone. The only thing I knew to do was pray, so I dropped to my knees in despair and asked God to send you back to me."

"Sweetheart, your prayers have been answered, but I'm so sorry you had to go through all that alone. I know you were afraid and heartbroken."

"Kit, I'm so glad you're here. Separation will never occur again. Hold me close and let us cherish this newness of life now and forever."

The Creator had found an inkling of uncertainty and had sent me back for a few moments to find out my belief in the truth, harmony, and understanding of my fellow man. God seemed satisfied with me and had granted us everlasting love and life. I had found my identity and destiny in a world unshaken by charisma and a will to succeed.

Lambda Photon and I will be forever joined in the tranquility of a new beginning for all people of the universe. Our joys will be a beacon in the heavens to guide every person in his individual search for the fulfillment of life itself.

I had cast my shadow on a lonely and uncharted island in space only to be christened into the salvation and redemption that accompanies life.

Our journey ended. We found not only the end of time, but a newness of purpose and enrichment only exceeded by the profound hearts and unselfish desires of human nature.